All-Star Pride

Orca sports

Sigmund Brouwer

Orca Book Publishers

Library and Archives Canada Cataloguing in Publication
Brouwer, Sigmund, 1959-
All-star pride / Sigmund Brouwer.
(Orca sports)

First published: Dallas: Word Pub., 1995.

ISBN 10: 1-55143-635-3 / ISBN 13: 978-1-55143-635-7

I. Title. II. Series.

PS8553.R68467A64 2006   jC813'.54   C2006-903490-7

Summary: There's plenty of money to be made…if he's willing to pay the
price for it.
First published in the United States by Orca, 2006
Library of Congress Control Number: 2006929012

Orca Book Publishers gratefully acknowledges the support for its publishing
programs provided by the following agencies: the Government of Canada
through the Book Publishing Industry Development Program and the Canada
Council for the Arts, and the Province of British Columbia through the BC Arts
Council and the Book Publishing Tax Credit.

Cover design by Doug McCaffry
Cover photography by Getty Images

ORCA BOOK PUBLISHERS   ORCA BOOK PUBLISHERS
PO Box 5626, STN. B   PO Box 468
VICTORIA, BC CANADA   CUSTER, WA USA
V8R 6S4   98240-0468

www.orcabook.com
Printed and bound in Canada.
Printed on 100% PCW recycled paper.
11 10 09 08 • 5 4 3 2

Other books by Sigmund Brouwer

*Rebel Glory, Tiger Threat,
Timberwolf Chase, Timberwolf Revenge,
Sewer Rats, Wired*

chapter one

Strangers don't smile at me. Even though I'm only seventeen, I'm too big to get smiles. I'm too wide. My nose is too squashed from being broken too many times. I give myself my own crew cut with hair clippers once a week because it saves me money at the barbershop. In other words, I'm about as pretty as my nickname: Hog—as in Hog Burnell, junior hockey player, hoping to make the big step from the Western Hockey League into the National Hockey League.

Since strangers never smile at me, I had no idea what to do as I walked down the aisle toward the back of the airplane. There were rows and rows of passengers. Each row faced the front of the airplane, so all the passengers faced me as I made my way past them. Row by row, everyone who was awake smiled at me.

I knew all those smiles weren't something I was imagining. I don't have an imagination. That's not my job.

My job is to skate as hard and fast as anyone in the WHL. My job is to pound all opposing forwards and defensemen into the boards whenever possible. My job is to score goals on those few times I have the puck and the net is so wide open that even an elephant in handcuffs couldn't miss.

So if it wasn't my imagination, why were all these people smiling at me as I headed for the restroom at the back of the airplane?

Maybe my zipper. I had been in the air— along with the rest of the guys on the team— for six hours, on the way to Moscow. I had managed to lay my head back in the cramped seat and sleep some. I had only woken up because I needed to go to the bathroom. Maybe, after rising to stretch in the aisle, I had broken my zipper.

I checked. Nope. My zipper was fine.

I kept moving. People were still smiling, and the aisle of the airplane seemed to stretch forever. What was I supposed to do? Smile back at them?

Not a chance, I decided. Smiling was not part of my job either.

I walked faster—not only because I didn't like the smiles, but also because I had important business at the back of the plane. The very important business that had woken me.

Walking faster only brought me quickly to a blond flight attendant in a blue uniform. She was serving coffee from a cart that blocked the aisle. I had to stand and wait behind her.

On the other side of the flight attendant, I saw an old lady in a black dress lift her head and stare at me. She elbowed her husband in the ribs and said something to him in a language I couldn't understand. Probably Russian. The raisin-faced man turned his eyes in my direction—and smiled.

What was going on?

The aisle seemed like a tunnel in a dream, where you're running like crazy but not getting anywhere.

It didn't help that I needed to reach the back of the plane so badly that I was ready to tap-dance in the aisle. Two other passengers, headed the same direction as I was, jammed the aisle behind me.

The flight attendant probably heard me grunt as I tried not to tap-dance. She turned, still holding a pot of coffee. Her eyes were about level with my chest. She had to tilt her head back to get a look at my face. She smiled too.

"I can see you obviously need to get past me," she said. Was it the tears of pain running down my face?

"That would be very nice, ma'am. Thank you."

Her eyes widened a bit, as if she was surprised someone as big as me could be polite. Poor, but proud and polite—that was the way my family had raised me on our prairie farm.

The flight attendant pushed the serving cart toward the back of the airplane. I followed close behind.

Every single person who looked up smiled at me.

I just gritted my teeth and pushed on. I finally got past the flight attendant and reached the restrooms at the back of the airplane.

Naturally, both were occupied.

I moaned a quiet moan. I tapped my foot.

"I see you're a hockey player," a man said from somewhere near my shoulder.

If I'm not good at smiling at strangers, I'm even worse at talking to them. He must have guessed from the hockey jacket I was wearing.

"Yes," I said, turning to see a middle-aged guy in blue jeans and an expensive sweater. I know how much good clothes cost. Someday, if I made it into the NHL, I would have a closet full myself. Nothing but the best money could buy.

"Part of a team?" he asked.

I could see the top of his head. One of the things I don't like about being tall is having to see the tops of people's heads. Especially those of middle-aged men. You can always tell when they're slicking their hair forward to hide baldness. Or worse, you see their dandruff like sugar sprinkles on a cake.

"Yes," I said, "part of a team."

But I was thinking, If you play hockey, you play on a team. That's what hockey is. A team sport. How obvious could it be? I didn't say it though.

"The team's going to Moscow?"

"Yes." Where else was this plane headed? Timbuktu?

"But this is summer," he said. "Hockey in the summer?"

"It's an all-star tour," I said. "Seven games in ten days against the Russian all-star team."

"Great! Go U.S.A!" he cheered.

"This all-star team has U.S. and Canadian players," I explained.

"I see." The guy was staring up at my crew cut as he talked, and it seemed like he was doing his best not to smile. I nearly told him that if I could afford a real haircut, I would get one. It was none of his business, though, why I worked so hard to save every penny I made.

"Well," he said a few seconds later, "part of a hockey team. That explains it, doesn't it?"

One of the restroom doors opened. A little girl walked out. Her head banged my knee, but she shook it off and walked up the aisle to find her mother.

"Yes, sir," I said to the guy as I turned to walk in. "I guess that explains it." Even though I had agreed with him, I was wondering what it explained. I thought the guy was crazy—until I walked into the restroom.

Then I saw why everybody had been smiling. Then I understood why the flight attendant had said it was obvious I needed to get past her. Then I realized why the middle-aged man had stared at my crew cut and said being on a hockey team explained it.

In the mirror, I stared at a pile of white shaving cream perched on my head. A big pile of white shaving cream. A big, quivering pile of white shaving cream. I looked like a human ice-cream cone. A human ice-cream cone who had just walked past every single person on the airplane with a stupid pile of light and fluffy shaving cream on top of his head.

I slapped the shaving cream off and toweled my hair dry. I slammed the door open and stomped down the aisle back toward my seat.

I'd heard enough about his practical jokes to know that no one but the Portland Winter Hawks' star center, Chandler Harris, would have put the shaving cream on my head while I was sleeping. I didn't care that he was a veteran of this all-star team. I didn't care that I was a rookie.

Chandler Harris needed to find a parachute and a quick exit. Or we were going to have a very uncivilized discussion, very soon.

chapter two

Because I have a temper and know I need to control it, I forced myself to take ten deep breaths. It gave me a chance to decide not to very publicly kill Chandler Harris. Our coach, Mel Jorgensen, was only two seats ahead of him. I hardly knew the coach, since all of the players had just been thrown together from different WHL teams for this tour. I didn't want his first impression of me to be a bad one.

Instead, when I got back to the front of the airplane I squatted in the aisle beside Harris. I looked straight into his green eyes. His sandy hair was slicked back, almost dark with hair gel. He wore a denim shirt, along with a tie. Team rule: Wear ties in public.

"Harris," I said.

He was laughing. So were most of the other guys in the seats nearby.

"Harris," I said again. Still squatting, I grabbed the front of his shirt and twisted it in my right hand. I didn't think I could lift him with just one arm, so I pulled him toward me and got my left hand on his shirt too.

"Hey, rookie, back off."

Rookie or not, I had pride. "I don't like losing my temper," I said.

"Rookie, I just told you to back off."

"People six foot seven and 250 pounds should never lose their tempers," I explained with a calm voice. "It can be unhealthy for everyone involved."

He didn't have much laugh left. I had no idea what the other guys on the team were thinking or doing. Chandler Harris had my total concentration.

I straightened from my squat. As I straightened, I began to lift him from his seat. He was a big hockey player; I was just a lot bigger.

Harris brought his hands up and grabbed my forearms. It didn't help him. I lifted him higher.

I stopped halfway up. No sense pulling him entirely out of his seat and letting everybody on the airplane see this. I held him there, with a lot of clear space between him and the seat below.

It took effort. But I pretended it didn't as I smiled into his green, wide-open eyes.

"Save your jokes and pranks for other people," I said.

I set him down gently and went back to my seat.

No one bothered me during the rest of the flight to Moscow.

We arrived at 10:00 AM local time, which gave us most of the day to rest before our

11

first game that evening. We were greeted in Moscow by scowling gray clouds outside the airplane window, and then by scowling gray men in dark suits who checked our passports, and finally by one pretty girl with a clipboard in her hands.

"Good morning to all," she said. Her accent made it sound like she was chopping her words.

The team listened; we had lined up near the conveyor belt that was spitting out our suitcases and duffel bags.

Coach Jorgensen was with us too. He was tall, with a sagging tired face and strands of hair combed sideways across his nearly bald head. He wasn't really paying attention to the girl with the clipboard.

The rest of us listened without moving. It had been a long flight on a cramped airplane. We were eleven time zones away from the western Canadian provinces and western United States. Our bodies said it was nighttime, but the clocks said we should get ready for a long day. Only a few of us mumbled greetings back.

"I am your tour assistant," she said. "My name is Nadia. Here in Moscow I work for the world's greatest museum, the Tretyakov Gallery, where I interpret for English tourists. My job is to escort your team over the next ten days of your tour."

Chandler Harris shuffled close beside me and nudged my ribs. "She won't be hard to look at, will she?"

I wondered why Chandler was trying to be friendly. I just grunted in reply because I sure didn't feel like being friendly to him. But in my mind, I had to agree. Nadia had hair as black as a raven that fanned out on the shoulders of her long raincoat. She had high cheekbones and a wide smile. She actually made me wish I had the kind of face that would give her an excuse to smile at me.

"There are some very simple rules," she was saying with her nice wide smile. "As you probably know, our country has been going through many changes. While we do welcome visitors, our laws are stricter than those of your home country. You must

13

stay in your hotels after 9:00 PM. Away from the hotel, you must at all times stay together with the other members of your team. And you must keep with the schedule we have set for you."

She waited to see if we had any questions. We didn't. We were too tired.

"Good then," she said. "In the event you need a translator, you may ask me for help."

She pointed beyond us to the doors that led outside. "Please collect your luggage. You will follow me to the bus outside."

This didn't sound like the summer vacation I had hoped it would be, and I must have been frowning.

"Don't sweat it," Chandler Harris said to me. "Think of all the money you'll make."

"If we win our series," I replied. That was how this exhibition tour had been set up: winner take all, with the prize money to be split among the players.

"That's right. If we win the series." Chandler winked at me as he picked up his duffel bag with his left hand and got ready to step into the line ahead of me. "But that's not what I meant, Hog. There are other ways to make money here. Tons more money."

"What do you mean?" I asked.

Chandler reached into his pocket with his right hand. Then he pulled his hand loose and extended it to me. "Shake hands, bud," he told me.

Reluctantly, I put my hand out. I didn't trust this guy.

He put his hand into mine. Then he pulled his hand away, leaving several folded pieces of paper in the palm of my hand.

"It's five hundred dollars, my friend," he said with another wink. "It's only a start. Trust me. It's only a start."

He walked away before I could say another word.

chapter three

We played our first game that night in a Moscow arena so old and dark that as we skated around our half of the ice during warm-up drills, I expected to see bats diving in and out of the rafters above us.

Old and dark arenas, I guessed, didn't bother Russians. The place was packed with fans, all cheering loudly for the Russian all-stars who circled the other half of the ice wearing maroon and black uniforms.

I skated along the boards, continued behind our net and slowed down as I came around the other side. I let myself slowly drift up the ice toward the centerline. I wanted a good close-up look at these Russian skaters.

They were slick, shifting and sliding as they passed the puck around. Their goalie looked sharp too as he bounced to his knees and popped back up again to make save after save on warm-up shots coming at him from all angles.

I reached the centerline and had to turn hard to keep from going into the Russian half. I skated slowly along the centerline toward the other side of the rink, trying to learn as much as I could about these Russian all-stars cruising around their end of the ice.

I was looking hardest for their big players. These were the guys I wanted to force into the boards first. Clean, legal body checks, of course. I didn't want a reputation as a goon. Besides, I didn't need to play dirty. I could do enough damage without getting penalties. If I could scare their biggest players early with that little damage, it would make it a lot easier for our team to win the series. And easier for me to collect my share of the $100,000 prize money.

I saw three players I decided I would need to work on: numbers 9, 23 and 28. Until I got beside them, I wouldn't know for sure how big they were, but it seemed like each would be a couple of inches shorter than I was.

Would they be tough?

I wouldn't know until the referee dropped the puck to start the game. I half-hoped they would be. I looked at the clock on the scoreboard. Just a few minutes left of warm-up skating.

The crowd began to chant a song I didn't recognize. Not that I expected to recognize anything. This was Russia. They were Russians. They were the enemy—if you listened to my dad—Commies, short for Communists.

Back home, I knew my high school history teacher would be having a fit if he knew I was calling them Commies. He'd tell me that the Communist government had ended and this was a new era, that Russians were now our friends.

Although I knew I should think of them as Russians, it wasn't easy. My dad had called them Commies ever since I could remember. We lived on a farm, and Dad hated it when the Russian government was allowed to buy wheat from us at low prices. His attitude had worsened since a farm accident put him in a wheelchair. It drove him nuts when he saw the Russian teams play hockey during the Olympics.

"Look at those Ruskies!" he would shout in our tiny living room as he pointed at the portable black-and-white television, which was all we could afford. "Look at those Commies! They take money out of our pockets by stealing our wheat! And now they're trying to take jobs from our boys by breaking into the NHL! Get me out of here! I can't stand to be in the same room with them!"

Of course, I knew if I even touched my dad's wheelchair to move him away from the television, he'd yell just as loudly at me. Dad loved to hate the Commies. So when the

Russians played hockey, instead of wheeling Dad away, I'd just pull up a chair and sit beside him. I'd listen to him yell the entire game, and I'd dream about the day I might play hockey on television too.

Now I was here, with less than five minutes remaining in warm-up. Television cameras had been placed high up in the stands of the arena, ready to catch the action of game one in this all-star series. I was here to play hockey. But thoughts of Chandler kept creeping into my mind. Why had he given me that money for no reason at all? I told myself to set aside my questions and concentrate on the game.

I was playing on the second line of this all-star team. I didn't get onto the ice until the referee stopped the play for a routine offside call against the Russians. The first line—led by Chandler Harris—skated off the ice into our players' box. We skated on. Jeff Gallagher from the Kamloops Blazers at center, Miles Hoffman from the Saskatoon Blades at right wing, and me from the Red Deer Rebels at left wing. Nathan Elrod from the Tri-City

Americans and Adam Payne from the Seattle Thunderbirds covered the defense positions.

I looked for my first target as we got into position for the face-off. I found him.

The Russian number 23 had the name Klomysyk across the back of his sweater. He played right wing. I played left wing, going the opposite direction. Which meant we lined up against each other during the face-off. My goal was to make Klomysyk feel like he'd lost a head-on collision with a locomotive—enough times so he'd learn to hate going into the boards to battle for the puck.

I glanced into his eyes as we waited for the referee to drop the puck. Beneath the half-shield visor across his face, sweat ran from his forehead into his eyebrows. His face was nearly as ugly as mine. We were the same height. His eyes were blank as we stared at each other.

I smiled my warrior smile.

The ref dropped the puck.

Their center managed to knock the puck back to his right defenseman. He in turn passed it across to the left defenseman. The

21

entire Russian team backpedaled as the two Russian defensemen continued to pass the puck back and forth.

Jeff charged ahead and pressed hard, almost knocking the puck from one defenseman, who again slid it across to the other defenseman. Miles cut quickly toward center, not quite intercepting the cross-ice pass between the Russians. I stayed back, giving Klomysyk room, but watching him closely.

Their other defenseman snagged the puck. I saw his head turn as he checked out his options. He saw Klomysyk open. Or he thought he saw Klomysyk open.

I practice judging how much room I can give without losing my guy completely. Maybe it's like playing cornerback in football. You want to tease the quarterback into thinking the receiver is open, only to find the juice to step up and intercept the ball.

It's risky. In football, the safer play is to cover the receiver so completely the quarterback looks for a better target. At the very least, you should try to just knock the ball down if the pass is made, because if you miss the interception, it's good-bye and lights out. The receiver will be on his way to an easy touchdown while you're still looking at your hands and wondering what happened to the football.

In hockey, it's not quite as risky to make your man look open. If I missed, he wouldn't have a sure goal. But he'd be past me, probably with a couple of other guys, and in a good position to put real pressure on our defensemen. Not only that. To me it's a matter of pride that I never miss.

I didn't this time.

The Russian defensemen fed the puck up-ice to Klomysyk, who was cruising along the boards. I timed it so my legs were in full speed. Just before the puck reached Klomysyk, I was already moving like a buffalo with its tail on fire.

Klomysyk put his head down briefly to watch the puck come to his stick. That was the moment I hit him. Full shoulders. Full hips. Full body contact at warp speed.

He was one big Russian. He was so solid that for a moment I wondered if

I'd hit him or if I'd missed and hit the boards.

Then I heard the grunt of the air leaving his lungs as he collapsed like a popped balloon. He fell to his knees. I stood above him. The puck squirted to Adam Payne.

Jeff and Miles hadn't made it back yet, so they were still up the ice and wide open for a pass from Adam. Adam fired it to Jeff, who was busting toward the Russian net and cutting between the two defensemen. The puck landed perfectly on Jeff's stick, and in that flash of time we had our first breakaway.

I didn't move from where I stood over the fallen Klomysyk. I just watched and grinned as Jeff pulled the puck left, faked a backhand, pulled it back to the right and lifted the puck over the diving goalie.

One to nothing for us!

Klomysyk pushed himself to his feet, glared at me and said some loud, fast words in Russian.

I just smiled. It was nice to know when a person was appreciated for his good work.

chapter four

A knock on our hotel room door woke us up for breakfast the next morning. My roommate for this tour, Nathan Elrod, bounced out of his bed and began dressing. Nathan had curly red hair. He was short and very wide, a fast skater with good hands who scored plenty of goals. This was his second year on the all-star tour to Russia. But at this moment—wearing boxer shorts decorated with Valentine hearts—he looked like anything but one of the leading goal scorers in the WHL.

I stayed in bed, turned my gaze to the ceiling and thought about the five hundred dollars I'd placed beneath my pillow before falling asleep. Since I had gotten the money from Chandler Harris at the airport, we'd been in a whirlwind. Bus to this hotel. A four-hour nap before last night's game. Bus back to the hotel right after the game. An entire night's sleep. I hadn't had a chance to talk to Chandler privately. As soon as I could, though, I would give him the money back.

"You played a great game last night," Nathan said from the other side of the room. He was hopping, with only one leg in his pants. "Or did I already tell you that as we were falling asleep last night?"

"Only about a dozen times," I said as I slid out of bed. "But you're welcome to say it another dozen times."

I was glad to have Nathan as a roommate. Before we'd each been traded, we'd played together briefly on the Kamloops Blazers. More than a couple of times, we'd had late-night conversations on long bus trips. Serious discussions you never had in the locker room.

Meaning-of-life discussions and questions about God and things like that, which seem easier to talk about when it's dark and quiet and the highway is humming beneath the bus wheels.

"You were nailing Russians left and right," he said, grinning. "They didn't have a chance."

"It did feel good," I said. "So did the 4-0 win. I hope we can keep it going and win tonight."

Nathan pulled a T-shirt over his head.

"By the way," he said as his head popped into sight again. "Make sure to take your food bag down to breakfast with you."

"Why? Won't it be easier just to take what I need?"

Every guy on the team had arrived with three pieces of luggage. A suitcase with clothes for ten days of travel. A duffel bag filled with hockey equipment. And a food bag, almost as big as the duffel bag, filled with cereal, granola bars, jars of peanut butter, cans of mixed nuts, and other assorted foods that wouldn't go bad without refrigeration. We'd each been told—actually ordered—to fill a bag because it was the best way to make sure you didn't starve or get sick.

"Why? So the hotel maids don't steal from it. We're in Russia. You take everything of value with you everywhere you go. Wallet, watch, Walkman, Game Boy."

I pulled on my pants. I didn't have a Walkman or a Game Boy. Just an empty wallet, a cheap watch and five hundred dollars to return to Chandler Harris. "Get out of here. Maids can't just walk in our hotel room and steal."

"I'm serious." Nathan was fully dressed now. "This is my second year on the tour, remember? People are desperate here. Poor. You should know that just from how bad the showers work. And this is one of the better hotels."

Cold, dribbling water was the best our shower would do, which was why we had both skipped it.

I shrugged. "I'll take your word for it."

I finished dressing.

Nathan grinned at me as I picked up my food bag. "By the way," he said, "if it's anything like last year's tour, I think you'll find breakfast quite interesting."

It didn't take me long to discover what he had meant. We walked into the large room that our team would use as an eating area. Cheap folding chairs had been set behind long wooden tables. The tables were bare, except for cutlery, empty bowls, and bottles of cola, already opened.

I took my seat beside Nathan.

"What's this?" I asked him. "Where's the milk? Juice? Water?"

"Like I said, this is Russia. You can't drink the water, you might get sick. Same with the milk, even when it's not sour. And juice is too expensive."

He searched through his food bag for a box of cereal. It rattled his bowl as he poured. Then he took a bottle of cola and dumped it over the cereal.

"You'll get used to it," he said between bites. "It's better than eating cereal dry. And lots better than getting sick and spending hours on a toilet or, more gross, leaning over a toilet and—"

"I get the message," I said.

"The worst thing is they think it's special service to open the bottles ahead of time. So not only is the cola warm, but it's also flat."

"Great."

He watched me pour cola into my bowl.

"Bon appétit," he said, "and welcome to hockey in Russia."

I caught up to Chandler Harris as we were filing out of the breakfast area. I pulled him aside in the hallway so we could speak privately.

"I need to talk to you about the money," I said. "I can't keep it."

He stared at me as if I were crazy. "You can't use five hundred dollars?"

"Not when I haven't earned it."

"You will," he said.

That set off major alarm bells in my head. "How?"

"You'll find out."

"I don't think so. I'm giving it back to you." I reached into my pocket and brought out the wad of money. I held it out to him.

Chandler put his hands on his hips and stared me straight in the eyes. He wore the grin he always gave goalies after scoring on them—a mean, teasing grin. "If you don't want it, Hog, throw it out. Dump it down a toilet. Give it to beggars. Or drop it here in the hallway for the next person to pick up. I don't care. I'm not taking it back."

Without another word, he walked away from me.

Fine, I told myself. I won't throw it out. I won't dump it down the toilet. Or give it to beggars. Or leave it here in the hallway. I'll keep it until I find out what he wants me to do to earn it. And then I'll tell him no and give the money back.

chapter five

"Listen up, guys," Coach Jorgensen said.

We listened. With about thirty minutes left until the start of the second game against the Russians, we were in various stages of equipment and uniform readiness in the dressing room. But we stopped our chatter and gave full attention to the man who had just walked in.

I had a small propane blowtorch in my hand. I had just lit it and was preparing to heat up the aluminum shaft of my hockey stick.

Some players preferred to use a traditional wooden stick. I couldn't. I tended to snap the shafts too easily. The aluminum shafts lasted longer. Only trouble was I often needed to replace the wooden blades , and the only way to do that was to heat the aluminum with a blowtorch to loosen the blade insert.

When Matthew Martin Henley walked into the dressing room, I adjusted the valve on the blowtorch so that the blue flame barely showed and barely hissed. It would save me time relighting the flame later. I set it nearby on the floor.

Because he had flown in the first-class section on our way here, this was my first good look at Matthew Martin Henley, the tour promoter who had put this series together. Henley had his hair spiked, shiny and short. His face was red and sweaty. He was fat and wore a three-piece navy blue suit. Although he had an unlit cigar in his mouth, ashes from previous cigars were sprinkled down the front of his navy blue suit. Not that I would let him know what I thought about his appearance. Matthew Martin Henley was the one who would be signing my paycheck if we won this series against the Russians.

"Last night's game wasn't bad," Henley said. He plucked the unlit cigar from his mouth and waved it around in his fat fingers like a baton, slashing the air to emphasize his words. "But it wasn't good enough."

Not good enough? We'd shut them out four to nothing. What more did he want?

"This ain't no charity tour," Henley told us. "You guys probably got that figured out. Every penny of your expenses and every penny of prize money comes out of my wallet."

He paused to dig in his pockets and came out with a heavy silver lighter. He waved his unlit cigar some more, as if he'd forgotten about the lighter he had just grabbed. "It works the same as last year. Our video crew patches the highlights together to make a one-hour special. Sure, the tour has seven games. What's that? Seven hours of ice time? Figure it out, guys. Seven hours cut down to one. Only the best hockey gets put on tape. And last year's special got good ratings. Real good ratings. You think it would hurt your pro career to get a big chunk of that hour on television? What I'm saying is each one of you should be trying to be a big hero and get your cut of the prime-time action."

He coughed and wheezed. Talking so much must have taken too much of an effort. I looked at his huge belly covered with enough navy blue material to make suits for three regular-sized men. I wondered when Henley had last been able to see his feet.

Matthew Henley brought the lighter up and jammed the cigar in his mouth. He flicked a flame and drew hard on the cigar, rolling it in his mouth to light it evenly. When he finished, he held the cigar up to admire it, then blew smoke into the center of the dressing room.

"So what I'm saying is it isn't good enough just to win. I want you guys passing the puck less."

Less? This was a team game. I glanced at Coach Jorgensen to see how he was taking it. After all, Henley had just marched in and given us orders, something that was supposed to be the coach's job. Coach Jorgensen simply stared at the ceiling. Obviously Matthew Henley signed Jorgensen's paycheck as well.

"You heard me," Henley said. "Less passing. Carry the puck more. I want some tough, gritty hockey. I want some great clips for the television special."

He grinned at us through a blue haze of cigar smoke. "Boys, don't think of this as hockey. Think of it as entertainment."

I was beginning to understand. Mainly because of what Nathan had earlier explained to me about this tour.

Matthew Henley and his financial partners backed all of it. Our expenses. The camera crew's expenses. The cost of renting each ice arena. The hundred thousand dollars in prize money for the team that won the best-of-seven series—two games here in Moscow, three scheduled in St. Petersburg, followed by a final two games back in Moscow.

Apparently it had taken a lot of wheeling and dealing for Henley to put the first tour together three years earlier. First, he'd had to convince the Western Hockey

League to let him approach a selection of all-star players. He had promised the league would get excellent prime-time exposure on television, plus a percentage of the profits.

His second step had been to sign up WHL players. That wasn't difficult. We knew we would split the prize money. Our team had twenty players. If we won, it meant five thousand dollars to me. While the guys in the NHL made much more serious money, for us players, one step below, a chance at five thousand dollars for only seven days of playing seemed like a good deal, especially since we would have played for nothing—just to be able to play. It didn't hurt, either, that the high visibility of the series might help us make the NHL some day.

Henley, in fact, would have preferred to put together an all-star team from the NHL— even if it would have cost him ten times as much. But he had found it impossible; all the players were bound by contracts and couldn't play for anyone else in the off-season. We WHL juniors, of course, didn't have those kinds of worries, although we all hoped for and dreamed about the day we would.

After getting commitments from the all-stars in North America, Henley had gone to Russia and convinced them to put together a junior all-star team. Not only did he promise them a chance at the prize money, but he also gave them all the gate receipts from spectators. Nathan had explained that the Russian players couldn't divide the money like we did. Instead, it would support the team in its travels to different tournaments around the world during the rest of the year.

Nathan had also informed me that Henley had invested close to five hundred thousand dollars. I'd whistled. A half-million dollars.

I'd asked why Henley and his partners would spend so much.

Nathan had solemnly said just one word: television.

Matthew Henley called this the *East Versus West Shootout*, and he reduced all seven games into a fast-paced one-hour hockey extravaganza. This television special would be released three months from now, in September, right when viewers were itching to see hockey again after the summer without it.

Henley had already sold his special to Canadian, American and European television networks for a big profit. The networks, in turn, sold advertising space and made an even bigger profit.

"You got me, boys?" Henley was saying. "You ain't hockey. You're entertainment."

He waddled close to where I was sitting and looked down at me. "You're Burnell, right?" He shook his head. "Don't take no offense, kid. I can't figure any of you out unless I got a program in my hand and you got numbers across your shoulders."

"I'm Burnell," I said. I could smell strong cologne. It had to be real strong to get past the raunchy cigar in his hand.

"Burnell. It's what I figured." He raised his voice for the rest of the guys. "I want more of you laying out hits like Burnell did to that kid last night. Hits look real good on television. And they don't hurt your chances of winning none."

He took a couple more puffs. "That's all I got to say for now."

He left us in a cloud of smoke. I reached for the blowtorch and twisted the valve to extend the flame. I was glad he had noticed me. I'd find out later that was a stupid thing to be glad about.

chapter six

I nearly killed myself attempting my first hit of the game. Henley had me so pumped and ready to perform that I was drooling at the prospect of a spectacular body check for the television cameras.

It was halfway through my second shift on the ice. Their defenseman had taken the puck behind the Russian net. I was forechecking hard. So was Miles, my center.

Miles raced down the right side of the ice, turning hard to spook the Russian defenseman out from behind the net. The Russian hesitated and looked for a safe outlet to dump the puck. He didn't find one.

With Miles charging in, the Russian started skating to the left side of the ice. It took him away from the safety of the net and squarely into my sights.

He put the puck in his skates and tried covering up, pressing himself against the boards and waiting for the impact as I slammed him.

Dead meat, I said to myself. Dad's going to love seeing me crush this guy on television.

The Russian knew I was coming at him, of course. Wouldn't you hear a locomotive steaming in at full speed?

Unfortunately, he made a move I'd never seen before. Just as my body screened him from the referee, he turned his stick at an angle—stick blade jammed into the boards at ice level, the top end of his stick pointing directly at my stomach.

I couldn't do a thing about it. My momentum carried all 250 pounds of me into the stick at full speed. Except it wasn't a stick. It had become a spear. And I hit it so hard I knew I had just installed another belly button somewhere in the lower part of my back.

I fell back and flopped like a fish in the bottom of a rowboat. I couldn't breathe. I couldn't scream. I wanted someone to slam me over the head with an oar to put me out of my misery.

Roughly five years later, I was able to take my first breath. It took another five years for my second breath.

One of the Russian's hockey gloves had fallen from his hand as I'd spun his stick away from him. It lay on the ice, just out of my reach. I crawled over and scooped it toward me.

I heard Russian protests. I ignored them. My stomach was about to give its opinion on what I'd just done to it.

I brought his glove to my mouth. It wasn't that I had anything against the Russian defenseman. He'd suckered me, and I deserved the punishment for my carelessness. No, it was the fact that I didn't have the energy to pull my own gloves off. Nor the time. And I didn't want the embarrassment of putting my last meal all over the ice in full view of the television cameras—and thousands of Russian fans.

I found enough air for one more breath. Then I threw up into the Russian's glove.

They didn't take me off the ice to our players' bench. Instead, when I managed to stand and gasp out a lie that I was just fine, the referee and linesmen took me to the penalty box.

They had decided throwing up in someone else's glove deserved a two-minute penalty for unsportsmanlike conduct.

The Russians scored during the power play and never looked back. Final score: 5–2 for the Russians.

chapter seven

My first surprise that night after the game was to discover Chandler Harris in my hotel room.

"I don't get it," I said. "Where's Nathan? I thought he was my roommate for the tour."

"You're some kind of big, rookie. Boom, all those big hits. Even after woofing in that guy's glove. Maybe you don't score any goals, but you make it easier for the rest of us, even if we didn't win tonight."

Harris was unloading a suitcase onto the bed across the room from mine. I didn't like that. I also wanted to tell him he'd played a terrible game. If he'd hit the wide-open net on a few of the chances he'd had, we'd be one game closer to winning the series, one game closer to the money I could really use.

"Where's Nathan?" I asked again.

Finished with his suitcase, Harris stood with his hands on his hips and took a long, slow look around the room.

"This ain't exactly a palace suite, is it, kid?"

I also didn't like being called rookie or kid. Harris was maybe nineteen years old. He'd been on this tour each of the previous two summers. Seventeen or not, I'd played my share of hockey too. This evening's game had shown it. I didn't have to put up with his attitude.

"Where's Nathan?"

Chandler Harris sighed. He did it so loud and so long it was obviously a fake sigh. Another thing I didn't like.

He imitated me. "Where's Nathan? Where's Nathan?" Another sigh. "Burnell, is your brain so small it can only hold one thought at a time?"

I started taking deep breaths to hold my temper.

"Relax," he said. "Save your muscle flexing for tomorrow's game. Nathan and I got switched around by Henley. You want to go down the hall and argue with Henley?"

I did not want to argue with Matthew Martin Henley.

"Fine," I said. "You and Nathan got switched by Henley. I'll live with it. Good night."

I sat down on the bed, pulled off my shoes and let them fall on the floor.

Chandler Harris grinned at me. I didn't like his grin either. It was the grin of someone whose parents had a couple of thousand dollars to spare on braces to make the grin perfect. His grin, though, became a frown as he realized I was serious about going to sleep.

"Just like that? Good night? You don't want to talk about the game? Don't want to

talk about being a rookie hero on the tour?
Don't want to talk about what it's like in
Russia? Don't want to ask any more questions
about the money I gave you?"

"It's not my job to talk."

He laughed. "Around me it is. Boy, oh boy,
rookie, I can see you've got a lot to learn."

If I told him I didn't like being called
rookie, he would probably make a point of
calling me rookie as often as he could as a
way to challenge me. When that happened,
I would either have to fight him or let him
get away with it. Fighting is stupid, so I smiled
to keep him from knowing how much I
didn't like his name for me.

"Good night," I said. I did have a lot of
questions about the five hundred dollars. But
I can be stubborn. I was going to wait until
he asked me to do whatever he was going to
ask of me; then I'd tell him about the various
places he could stuff his money.

I was still sitting on the edge of the bed. I
leaned over to peel my socks off. As I looked
downward, pieces of paper floated onto the
carpet between my feet. They were green

pieces of paper. Twenty-dollar bills. I counted them without moving or picking them up. Twenty-five of them. Another five hundred dollars.

"Still thinking of sleepy time?" Chandler's voice had a rough edge to it, like he wanted to push me as far as he could.

"Good night," I said. I noticed, though, that I hadn't taken either of my socks off. Five hundred dollars.

"The money's yours," he said. "Plus the other money I gave you earlier. But you'll have to put your shoes back on. That's five hundred dollars per shoe."

I couldn't help myself. I nibbled at the bait. "Just for putting my shoes on?"

"And for going for a little walk around the block with me."

"Sure," I said sarcastically. "You're doing it for exercise."

"Don't worry about what I do," he said. "All you need to do is walk with me. Nothing else."

I looked at my watch. "It's already past the nine o'clock curfew. We're supposed to stay in the hotel. Besides, you don't speak Russian. I don't speak Russian. It would be stupid to wander around Moscow."

I still hadn't told him no, despite my earlier resolution. One thousand dollars was a lot of money.

Chandler Harris laughed again. Somehow it wasn't the kind of laugh that had anything to do with humor.

"Like I said," he told me, "you've got a lot to learn, rookie."

He looked at his own watch. "You pick up that money and fold it into your pocket. We've got less than a minute left."

"A minute left until what?"

"No questions. All you need to do is walk with me," he said. "Nothing else. Do you want the money or not?"

One thousand dollars. I thought of my dad watching his tiny black-and-white television from the wheelchair he could never leave. I thought of my mom collecting eggs every day. She sold them in town at the garden markets where city people kept knocking her prices down until what she made barely covered the cost of the gasoline it took to get into town.

One thousand dollars. I picked up the money and folded it into my back pocket. I'd go for the walk. Only for as long as I liked what was happening. If it turned out he expected me to do something illegal, I would definitely give it back to him then.

I had barely laced up my shoes before there was a soft knock at our hotel room door.

Chandler Harris grinned his perfect white grin. "What did I tell you? Just on time."

He opened the hotel door to let our visitor slip inside.

"Hog," he said, "maybe you and I can't speak Russian, but she can."

I lifted my eyes to look into the face of Nadia. Nadia with raven black hair. Nadia our tour guide. Nadia, who had made it plain on the first day that she didn't want anyone on the team leaving the hotel after nine o'clock.

chapter eight

Nadia no longer showed the wonderful wide, curving smile of a translator and tour guide. Instead, her face was pinched, as if she were angry. She wore a short leather jacket and blue jeans. Her hair was free and loose. She appeared much younger—and even prettier, if that was possible—than she did as a tour guide with a clipboard.

I looked at Chandler to see if he was going to explain this. Chandler ignored me. He returned to his suitcase and took out a small package, which he tucked inside his shirt.

"Let's go," he said to Nadia. Chandler jerked his thumb at me. "Gorilla here will be keeping us company."

Gorilla? That was far beyond calling me rookie or kid. I opened my mouth to tell him to apologize. I remembered the thousand dollars. I snapped my mouth shut.

Nadia shrugged. From her, it was an expression of poetry. I reminded myself to keep reminding myself that beautiful girls did not look twice at a face like mine.

Nadia opened the hotel room door and peeked down the hallway. Without looking back at us, she waved us forward. We followed her into the hallway and down to an exit door around the corner.

She pushed the door open to show a narrow stairway, lit by a bare lightbulb dangling from a cord. We stayed behind her as she led us up the stairs. It smelled like cats had used every second step as a litterbox.

She took us up three flights of stairs to another door that led to the roof. The door creaked open. After the cramped smelly stairway, the fresh night breeze seemed as sweet as air to a drowning man.

The entire time she had said nothing to us. She had simply walked with her shoulders square and her body rigid. More of a march than a walk, except her feet had made no noise during the angry march.

On the flat hotel roof, she remained silent. She led us across a mixture of gravel and tar to a waist-high ledge that ran along the edge of the hotel roof. It had rained earlier, and cars below on the busy streets splashed through a sheen of water on the pavement.

I looked around carefully. If I had counted right, we were six stories off the ground. Three stories up from our third-floor hotel room. The stone building immediately next to this one was two stories taller.

She pointed to a rickety fire escape stairway running down the outside of the other building.

"We go across to there," she said. "Then down and onto the street."

"No way," Chandler protested. "I can't jump that far. And there's no place to land."

As much as I tended to want to disagree with Chandler on anything, this was one time he was right. The gap across was double the length of a bed. And I couldn't see myself taking a running dive onto the fire escape on the outside of the other building.

Nadia gave a scornful toss of her hair. "Fool," she said, in a tone that made me glad it was Chandler, not me, she was talking to. "You think I am not prepared?"

She stooped, reaching into the shadows cast by the small ledge. That's when I noticed the ladder on the gravel and tar, laid flat along the edge of the roof.

"Set this across," she said.

Chandler shook his head.

I wasn't eager myself. It was a six-story drop into a dark alley below. And whatever they planned to do next was something I knew we shouldn't be doing. If I'd had any brains, I would have turned around and left.

But I had a feeling Nadia didn't want to be here either. After Chandler had called me a gorilla, I, too, had walked with square angry shoulders and lips pressed tight into silence. Maybe I was hoping something was forcing her to do whatever we were doing so that I could still think of her as sweet and innocent. Maybe I was hoping I could rescue her from whatever I wanted to believe was forcing her to do this.

Or maybe it just made me feel good to do something that Chandler obviously feared. I lifted the ladder and swung it out until the far end rested on a platform of the other building's fire escape stairway.

"Go-ree-la," she said to me in her thick Russian accent, "you will hold it strong for me?"

I nodded. I hoped she thought Gorilla was just another regular English name, like Michael or Jeremy.

Without hesitation, she climbed onto the ladder and began to crawl across. It was a long time for me to hold my breath, but she finally got to the fire escape.

"I can't do this," Chandler said. "I hate heights."

So did I, but he wasn't going to know it.

"You must do this," she called across. She was keeping her voice low. "We only have half an hour to the meeting."

"I can't," Chandler said. "I'll go another way. I'll take my chances getting caught downstairs in the hotel lobby."

"You are very small brained," she told him. I enjoyed hearing someone else get accused of being dumb. "You know there will be those watching for you."

"It's the heights! I can't!"

"Will you be able to walk with your knees broken?"

Chandler thought about it and took a deep breath. "Hold the ladder good," he told me.

I did. I was tempted to shake it when he got to the middle, as punishment for calling me gorilla. But I knew he would have his turn to hold the ladder for me.

He crossed and on the other side held the ladder for me. I made it across without plunging to my death on the pavement below.

While the trip across did bother me some, I was more worried about other things. Who were the people Nadia and Chandler expected to be watching us? And who was Chandler so afraid of that he had forced himself to cross the ladder rather than risk getting his knees broken?

chapter nine

It seemed like the twilight zone. Beggarwomen on street corners wore mufflers across their faces and stuck out bony hands to plead for money. Greasy-haired children with dead faces sat on the curbs of underpasses. Old men slept in doorways beneath strips of cardboard.

We walked for what seemed like hours until we came to a part of Moscow with abandoned warehouses. A line of bikers, each in a leather jacket, passed us and roared toward the warehouses on ancient motorcycles with no mufflers. Bumper to bumper, cars blocked all the streets leading to the warehouses.

"Black market," Chandler said. His voice no longer carried the teasing cockiness of an all-star hockey player. He was tense, nervous.

"Black market," I repeated. I felt like a sheep among wolves. Already I regretted keeping the money in my back pocket. But with all the twisting, crooked streets, I had no idea how to get back to the hotel on my own.

Chandler eased himself closer to me, walking in the shadow that my body cast as we moved from one dim streetlight to the next.

"Black market. The place where you can buy anything if you have American dollars."

Nadia stayed slightly ahead of us. She had been silent the entire way.

"Why are we here?" I asked.

"Shut up," he said. "Please just shut up and look big."

I can tell fear when I hear it. I almost felt sorry for him. I wondered what was in the package he had slipped beneath his shirt.

There were large open squares of pavement among the warehouses. Squares of pavement filled with vans, tables, canvas tents—lit by kerosene lamps, which filled the air with trails of black smoke.

It seemed like there were thousands of people among the vans and tables and canvas tents. Silent people. Hands jammed in their pockets as they surveyed the black-market goods and whispered offered prices.

I saw cartons of cigarettes stacked like brick walls. Box after box of bottles of vodka. Sides of beef hung inside a butcher's truck. Dresses on hangers filled a tent. A man unloaded DVD players and radios from the trunk of a black Mercedes. Gypsies wandered around with briefcases, opening them to show glittering gold watches to anyone interested.

Chandler followed so close to me that I was afraid if I stopped, he'd run into me and break his nose. Nadia led us in a straight line through the eerie gray silence of the huge marketplace. She slowed and spoke briefly over her shoulder. "Look no one in the eye; speak to no one. If they know you are from America, you stand a good chance of being killed. They think all Americans are rich. And it is easier to rob a dead body than a body that can fight or run."

She moved ahead.

Chandler crowded even closer to me as we followed.

Minutes later, two kids stepped out from behind a tent and grabbed Nadia by the shoulders.

She said something quick and low.

Their heads turned and they looked at me. They disappeared. Ugliness, I guess, has its benefits.

She continued to lead us through the throngs of people until we reached another Mercedes, parked in front of a warehouse, its engine running. This one was gleaming white with dark windows of smoked glass. It was impossible to see inside.

Nadia tapped on the window twice.

The window slid down a half inch, operated by electric controls inside. All I could see was the top of someone's head. Cigarette smoke drifted out and upward.

Nadia said something in Russian.

The person inside said something.

She replied.

The person inside grunted.

Nadia turned to Chandler. "Deliver it."

"Are you sure?" he asked. "I mean, if I make a mistake, I'm dead."

She froze him with a look of hatred.

Chandler reached into his shirt, pulled out the package and slipped it into the slight opening at the top of the window. The window slid up, the transmission clicked into gear and the car drove away.

The doorway of the warehouse was straight ahead, and with the car gone, I noticed a man in the shadows, watching us. I wondered if it was my imagination, or if the man actually wore an eyepatch. To me, with his dark goatee and the eyepatch, he looked like a pirate, waiting to pounce. I was glad when Nadia turned away and began to lead us back to the hotel.

chapter ten

After breakfast the next morning we loaded ourselves and all our luggage and equipment onto an old bus. Coach Jorgensen and Nadia fussed around, making sure we didn't forget anything or anyone.

After all the guys were on the bus, Coach Jorgensen took a seat near the front. I was beginning to learn that he generally did his best to ignore us, except during the games.

Nadia stood in the aisle beside him. She told us our destination was Leningradsky

Vokzal, the Leningrad train station. Not that I cared too much. The train would take us north to St. Petersburg. All that mattered to me was the third game of the series, which we would play there this evening. We needed the win to keep the Russians from getting too confident.

"You are most fortunate," she said, keeping her balance by clinging to a greasy chrome pole behind the driver. "We take the Avrora, a high-speed train. Our trip will be only six hours."

Six hours. I hoped Chandler Harris would find someone else to sit beside the entire way. He'd made sure to plop down beside me on the bus, winking at me as he'd pushed me toward the window to make room for himself. I wanted to tell him he hadn't bought me with that stupid thousand dollars. Instead, I had just bitten my tongue and stared out at the old brick and stone buildings of Moscow.

"Again," she said, "I cannot warn you too strongly of the importance of staying together as a team. Russia has made great strides

65

in welcoming tourists. However, there are many dangers."

No kidding, I told myself. Like trips after curfew that might end up killing a person. I didn't like any of this. I just didn't know how to get myself out.

Nadia happened to look at me as she was warning us about the dangers. For a moment her eyes locked with mine. Her face tightened and turned cold.

She moved her eyes away from mine and spoke to the rest of the team. "At the station, you will wait for me. I will purchase your tickets and show you which train to board."

She sat down beside Coach Jorgensen. The guys on the bus started talking among themselves.

"What about Matthew Henley and the camera crew?" I asked Chandler. Any subject but last night. I wanted to pretend it had never happened.

"Huh?" He was busy with some fishing line in his lap.

"Henley. The promoter guy. You know, the one who smokes cigars and drives us nuts?

And the camera crew. I don't see them."

"Oh, them." The cockiness was back in his voice. "Henley probably took a taxi to the train station. He always travels first-class, never with the team. And the camera crew guys always have to go the night before, to set up. In the old barns these Russians call ice rinks, it's a real nightmare trying to find power outlets and whatever else the camera crew needs for their equipment."

As Chandler spoke, he was using a needle to thread fishing line into a ten-dollar bill.

He caught me watching.

"Ten bucks," he said. "Worth around ten thousand rubles. When I first did this tour two years ago, ten bucks was only worth about one thousand rubles. Inflation is killing this country." He wrinkled his forehead. "You do know what inflation is, right? Or is your head just filled with muscle?"

I could have told him it was an increase in prices while money fell in value, something I remembered from my social studies class in high school, but I had a feeling it wouldn't hurt if Chandler thought I was dumb. I ignored his question and pointed at the money and the fishing line.

"Why?"

"You know me," he said. He grinned his evil grin. "Mr. Practical Joker. I like to have fun. Wait till we're at the train station and you'll find out. Trust me, this one never fails."

The train station smelled of oil and diesel fuel and cigarette smoke. Tracks ran right into the domed building of Leningradsky Vokzal, and I counted eight sets, six with waiting locomotives and attached passenger cars. One track had a train just leaving, and the other was empty. The signs around me had the funny characters of the Russian language. There was no way I could have found the train or even the time of our departure for St. Petersburg. Nadia was right. Without her, we would be in trouble.

Before going to get our tickets, Nadia directed us to some empty benches where we piled our equipment. Most of the guys sat. I stood near the end of one of the benches and began to look around.

For a huge building filled with thousands of people, the train station was surprisingly quiet. I couldn't figure it out until I had spent a couple of minutes watching the Russians as they flowed around us. Most of them kept their heads down, as if they were trying to blend in with the background. If they were walking with someone else, their conversations were low. I saw no smiles. Heard no laughter. It reminded me of a tour our high school class had taken through a penitentiary. Gray clothes and gray faces of men trying to be invisible as the guards watched them.

I sat down at the end of the bench and waited for Nadia to return.

A middle-aged man wearing a black suit and carrying a briefcase walked by. Suddenly he stopped, as if he'd been jolted with electricity. He looked around quickly to see if anyone was watching; then he bent over to pick something up. I leaned forward to see what it was.

I saw a ten-dollar bill on the marble floor. The same one he couldn't believe was his just for the taking.

The middle-aged man's fingers twitched as he plucked at the bill. Just before he reached it, it floated away and stopped a half-step beyond him. He moved forward and bent over again to pick it up . And, again, it floated away just before he could grab it.

He frowned and, still bent over, took another quick step forward, only to see the money float away from him a third time.

I heard snorting laughter from the guys around me. Then I figured it out. Chandler Harris, sitting in the middle of the bench with the guys on both sides of him, was reeling in the ten-dollar bill with the fishing line. The line itself was invisible in the low fluorescent light of the train station.

The middle-aged man must have heard the laughter too. He straightened, tugged at the bottom of his suit jacket, arched his shoulders and quickly walked away.

Chandler got up and placed the ten-dollar bill where it had been.

Now that the guys knew what to expect, they all leaned forward and watched and waited. It took less than a minute for someone else to notice. This time it was a greasy-haired kid a couple of years younger than us. Wearing a faded nylon jacket, he tried to look tough with a cigarette perched on his bottom lip. He, too, stopped as if jolted by electricity. He didn't look around to see if anyone was watching, though; he just made a quick grab for the money.

Chandler yanked it back. The greasy-haired kid stumbled after it. Chandler kept pulling it back. The kid fell to his knees trying to get it. Most of the guys on the team busted out in laughter.

The kid stood. He glared at us and did his mathematics. Twenty of us. One of him. He spit in our direction and walked away.

"Cool, Chandler," one of the guys said. "Do it again!"

Chandler walked out from the bench and set the ten-dollar bill back into place.

I didn't like watching it. For starters, I thought it was mean. But it also reminded me of the money Chandler had dangled in front of me. Not ten dollars, but one thousand dollars. I forced myself to keep my mouth shut.

Chandler did the trick to two other people. Another guy in a suit. And a newspaper vendor who dropped all his papers trying to pick up the ten-dollar bill.

Chandler's next victim was an old lady in a brown dress who leaned on a cane for support as she walked.

The old lady did what all the others had done when seeing the money on the floor. She stopped, unable to believe her good luck. She didn't bend over, though, not when she was so old it might have broken her back. Instead, she stabbed her cane down and pinned the money to the floor.

This time, I laughed. Served Chandler right, teasing innocent people like this.

I had underestimated Chandler, though. He showed patience. The old lady shuffled forward to pick up her prize. With great effort she squatted downward to get her money. During the brief moment when she lifted her cane to claim the bill, Chandler yanked the money away. The old lady nearly fell forward in surprise. She managed to totter upward and took a few more shuffling steps toward the money. By then, Chandler knew what to expect, and when she stabbed her cane downward to pin the money again, he yanked the fishing line.

She stabbed, he yanked. She stabbed, he yanked. Three more times she missed the money. Each time she almost fell with her effort.

She had her head down and was concentrating hard on chasing the ten-dollar bill. Her shuffling brought her right to our bench. Her hearing must have been bad because she didn't react to the laughter of the guys around Chandler.

She took a final stab at the money, so close to Chandler she almost got him in the toe. He was forced to reel the money upward into the air and almost into his lap.

She squawked at the sight of a paper bill rising into the air. It brought her head up, and she finally realized what Chandler had been doing.

She was so close I could see the bleary redness of her eyes. The wrinkles on her face bunched together, and she screeched with anger.

Chandler laughed. She swatted him across the top of his head with her cane.

"Hey!" he shouted.

She shouted back at him in Russian and whopped him across the head again.

He ducked and tried to cover his head with his hands. She took another swing and mashed the tops of his fingers. He yelped and pulled his hands away to save his fingers, and she hit him again across the top of the head.

By then, the rest of the guys were almost rolling on the ground with laughter.

"Grab her, guys," Chandler shouted. "Haul her away!"

She kept screeching in Russian and swatting him with her cane. People passing by ignored it. Chandler started to run. I guess even he couldn't bring himself to hit an old lady.

She tottered after him, whacking him across the back until he finally cleared the arc of her swinging cane.

I picked up the fishing line and the ten-dollar bill from where Chandler had dropped it in his hurry to escape. I ran after the old lady, who was still doing her best to catch up to Chandler.

I managed to get in front of her and hold out the money.

"Here," I said, "you earned it."

She glared at me. I started to explain again, then realized she didn't understand English.

I reached down with my other hand and grabbed her bony wrist. I turned her hand so her palm was up, and I placed the money in her hand.

She smiled, showing one tooth and a lot of gums.

I began to smile back, but then I froze. She was so tiny she barely reached my waist. I could see clearly over her head. And what I saw I didn't like.

It was the man with the goatee and the eyepatch. The man I had seen the previous night at the black market. He was near the window where Nadia had gone to get our tickets. And he was standing beside her, his hand on her shoulder, leaning down and whispering in her ear.

chapter eleven

From the opening minutes of game three in St. Petersburg, I felt like Arnold Schwarzenegger on skates. Nothing was going to stop me.

I played a dozen hard shifts in the first fifteen minutes of the game. I banged Russians into the boards each and every time they so much as sniffed at the puck on my side of the ice.

I knew I was doing a good job because every time I stepped onto the ice for another shift, the Russian crowd began to whistle at me, their way of booing. It wasn't the kind of loud whistling you do with your fingers in your mouth, but the soft whistle of putting just your lips together. With thousands of people whistling that way, it sounds almost scary.

I ignored them. I knew my job, and I was doing it. Although we hadn't yet scored, we'd kept steady pressure on the Russians, and they'd barely had a couple of shots on the net.

I felt good too. I was sweating freely, my lungs were huge air pumps and my muscles were loose and relaxed. I stepped onto the ice for another shift. The clock showed just over three minutes left in the first period.

The face-off was to the left of the net in our end, with our line the same as it had been since the beginning of the series. Jeff Gallagher was at center, Miles Hoffman at right wing, me along the boards at left wing. Nathan Elrod played left defense directly behind the face-off circle, and Adam Payne at right defense covered the front of our net.

The ref dropped the puck, and Jeff picked it clean out of the air, pulling it back to Nathan. He took the puck behind the net. Klomysyk, the giant right winger, charged after him. I waited along the boards, open in case Nathan decided to pass it in my direction.

He did.

Unfortunately, Klomysyk—between Nathan and me—got just enough of the puck to slow it down as it went past him. The puck wobbled and skidded as it trickled along the boards toward me.

Not good. I'd have to wait far too long for the puck to reach me.

It gave the Russian defenseman time to leave his position on the blue line and flash toward me. I knew he was coming, but there was nothing I could do except swing my body around and try to trap the puck in my skates. Better to hold on for another face-off than try to do something fancy and risk losing the puck.

I held my position at the boards and concentrated on keeping the puck trapped when the defenseman hit me. He bounced off my shoulders and took another run. It wasn't him I was worried about. I knew Klomysyk would return from behind our net and take a full charge at me in revenge for the hit I'd given him in game one.

Nathan later told me that Klomysyk had the butt end of his stick out about a mile when he hit me.

I didn't see it.

It felt like I'd been rammed by a rhino horn, followed by the rhino itself. Something brutally hard slashed across my right cheekbone, just beneath my protective visor. My head cracked into the glass above the boards, and I spun around and toppled face-first onto the ice.

I pushed myself up. I couldn't figure out why the ice below me was sticky and red. Then the pain hit, and I realized how badly I'd been cut.

I saw more red. Not the red of my blood—of which there was plenty spurting from a gash across my cheekbone—but the red of the temper I tried never to lose.

I roared as I scrambled to my feet.

There was a confusion of players all around, and I bellowed as I flung them aside. Wherever he was, Klomysyk was going to pay. I saw him on the other side of the linesman who had whistled the play down and was skating in to see if I was okay. It was wrong. Very wrong. But I roared again and charged toward Klomysyk.

The linesman put his hands up to stop me, then changed his mind and jumped aside.

I must have looked like Frankenstein's monster to Klomysyk, with my hands outstretched, my cheek slashed wide open, and blood on my mouth and neck and shoulders. Or it could have been my eyes. The guys told me later it looked as if my eyeballs had rolled into the back of my head and I was a man totally out of control.

Which I was.

Klomysyk backpedaled a few uncertain steps.

I was still roaring, still gaining speed, throwing my gloves off as I closed in on him.

Klomysyk turned his back on me and skated as fast as he could.

I chased, fueled by absolute rage.

Klomysyk took a peek over his shoulder and picked up speed. I might have been mad, but he was afraid for his life.

Fear proved to be faster than anger.

I chased him all the way to their end, all the way to his net.

He hid behind the goalie, who had moved a little way up the ice.

I threw the goalie aside as if he were made of Styrofoam.

Whatever Klomysyk saw in my eyes, it told him to do one thing.

With the goalie gone, he raced the few steps back to the net, grabbed the crossbar and fell to his knees at the same time. He pulled the entire net down on himself.

I couldn't stop my dive in midair, so I tumbled into the netting, trying to rip through the mesh to get at him.

That's where both linesmen and the referee finally managed to capture me—on top of the net trying to punch my way through the mesh to get at Klomysyk.

They pulled me away and dragged me back toward our players' box. Sanity finally returned, time slowed and I felt as stupid as I must have looked.

My bleeding didn't slow down, though. And there was a thin line of red splotches the length of the ice where I'd chased Klomysyk.

As they led me off the ice, Klomysyk finally decided it was safe to crawl out from beneath the net. The entire crowd whistled at him. A part of me wondered whether they whistled at him for the dirty shot he had given me or for hiding in the net.

The major part of me, however, was just trying to keep my balance as weakness hit me. During the intermission between the first and second periods, a doctor worked quickly on my face, taking thirty stitches to close the cut. Before the second period had even begun, the side of my face had ballooned so badly I couldn't see out of my right eye.

As much as I tried, I couldn't convince the coach or doctor to let me play the rest of the game. I was forced to sit in the stands, just above our players' box. More than a few Russian fans made a point of stopping by to shake their heads with sympathy, saying angry words that I guessed meant they were as disgusted with Klomysyk as I was.

It also made me feel a little better that my thirty stitches helped us during the second period. Klomysyk received a five-minute major penalty and a game misconduct. It meant we had a man advantage for all five minutes, and our team scored three goals while the Russians were shorthanded.

It didn't make me feel better, however, to see the guy with the goatee and the eyepatch again, here in St. Petersburg, six hours of high-speed travel away from Moscow. And it made me feel even worse to see him with Nadia. They were on the opposite side of the arena, high up in the stands where they were nearly invisible among the crowd of people.

I wondered why I felt so jealous to see him playing with her long hair and whispering in her ear. After all, I was nothing to her. And it was becoming obvious she was someone not to trust in any situation, let alone in a country where I could easily get lost and never be found again.

As the second period continued, however, I couldn't keep my eyes from constantly looking in her direction. We were up 4-1 with nine and a half minutes of play left in the second period when I glanced in her direction again.

The eyepatch guy had taken her by the elbow and was leading her up the aisle. At the top of the aisle, it looked like she tried to pull away from him.

He yanked her toward him.

She pulled back again.

So quickly I wondered if it had actually happened, the eyepatch guy slapped her across the face.

chapter twelve

Coach Jorgensen had told me to stay in the stands right above our players' box. He had told me to wait until the second period ended and then return to the dressing room to join the team.

But Coach Jorgensen's attention was on the game, not on me.

I spun out of my seat and dashed upward, away from the players' box. I pounded up the steps of the aisle. At the top, I turned right and sprinted through the oval concourse that would take me around to the other side.

Most of the spectators in the rink were in the stands, watching the game. The few Russians wandering throughout the concourse wisely moved aside as they saw me running. And it was probably a good thing too. Since the vision in my right eye was blurry and my balance was off, I'm not sure I would have been good at dancing around them, not at the speed I was running.

I didn't know what I was going to do or say when I reached Mr. Eyepatch, but I wasn't going to need Russian to let him realize what I thought about him hitting Nadia, especially if this involved the danger for her I thought it did. Whatever had happened in the black market could not have been good, and he was obviously connected with it, even if I didn't know how or why.

It probably took less than thirty seconds to make it halfway around the oval. I'm big but faster than I look. Even then, arriving so quickly, I was barely in time to see them.

Mr. Eyepatch had pushed Nadia through a double-wide exit door at the far end of the concourse. If the slap to her face hadn't been enough indication of trouble, this confirmed it. Nadia was supposed to always be near our team. Should any major incident take place, she would have to translate for us. So I guessed if she was leaving, it probably wasn't by her choice.

I started running again.

The crowd roared, and part of my mind told me the Russians had just notched a goal. I didn't spare the ice a glance.

I burst through the doors.

Sunlight battered my eyes. Although it was mid-evening, St. Petersburg was far enough north that, at this time of year, the days were so long the sun barely set for more than a couple of hours.

My head seemed filled with pounding blood. I wondered if any of my stitches had broken open. I blinked away the sudden light, heaving for breath. My right eye filled with tears. I rubbed the tears away, and when I was able to focus again, I saw the two of them rounding the corner of the outside of the building.

Again, like a fool, I rushed forward.

Unlike ice arenas and major stadiums in North America, this one did not have acres and acres of parking lots. Not enough Russians could afford cars. The tiny parking lot was deserted. I didn't have to worry about knocking anyone over.

I rounded the corner and ran into deep shadow. Buildings pressed in all around this ice arena, and I dashed forward into a narrow alley alongside the arena.

What a mistake.

Mr. Eyepatch stepped out from behind an old truck. At full speed, I almost speared myself on the huge knife he held waist high in my direction. I managed to throw myself to the side and dodge the knife.

I stopped a few stumbling steps later, turned to face him and gasped for breath.

He snarled something at me in Russian.

I didn't move. There were only those couple of steps between us. Up close, even in the shadows, I could see how his face was filled with pockmarks. His hair was short, lined with gray. The goatee, too, showed gray. The eyepatch covered his right eye. His left eye glittered black with hatred.

He snarled more Russian.

I couldn't think of anything to say. He held a knife; I didn't. Big as I am, the knife made up for a lot of his disadvantage in size. Especially the knife he held, a big bowie knife with notched ends.

He waved it at me and stepped forward.

I stepped back and bumped into some garbage cans.

Again, more nasty Russian, probably curses. More knife waving.

"Goreela," Nadia's voice floated out from beside the truck, "he asks why you have turned on him."

There was a slight scuffling, and she came into view. Two of her. My vision was blurring. I also saw two trucks, two of Mr. Eyepatch and, worst of all, two of the murderous knives.

"Tell him he shouldn't hit you." Wet warmth was running down my face and onto my neck. I realized it was blood from my stitches.

"You came out here because he hit me?" Her voice was filled with disbelief. "You risk everything for something as simple and meaningless as that?"

Simple? Meaningless? Why did she sound so old as she said it?

Mr. Eyepatch spoke to her without taking his glittering black eye off me.

She replied in Russian, explaining, I guessed, what each of us had just said.

He laughed. It sounded as mean and hollow as one of Chandler's laughs.

"Tell him to put that knife away before I get really, really mad," I said. I hoped my voice didn't sound as shaky as I felt.

"You simple boy," she told me. "Have you no idea what you've done?"

I had a good idea. Too good. I'd backed myself completely into a set of garbage cans. With a madman ready to rip my stomach apart. All for a girl who didn't seem too impressed that I had tried to defend her.

Mr. Eyepatch slashed the air in front of me.

I tried pulling back and knocked over a garbage can. It clattered on the pavement. He laughed again.

I had never felt more alone. I'd been raised on a farm and had learned how to be tough against the weather, against hard work, against the bitterness that had made my father hateful toward life. In hockey, I'd learned how to be tough against uncaring coaches, against opponents who wanted to crush me and against all the lonely hours of missing my family during the months on the road.

But I had never learned how to fight for my life.

Nadia shouted something at Mr. Eyepatch in Russian. Her voice sounded desperate. Was she begging him not to do this to me?

Another slash.

This time I fell backward. My vision was betraying me. With blurred vision in one eye, I had trouble getting my bearings.

He moved forward.

I kicked at his knee.

He laughed and jumped back.

I tried pushing up. In the rotted garbage

91

spread all around, my hand touched cool metal. The metal of a garbage can lid. I watched him close in on me. He was taking his time, licking his lips like a cat watching a crippled mouse.

I felt for the handle of the lid.

He moved forward again.

Nadia continued to plead with him in Russian.

I closed my fingers over the handle and jumped to my feet. He seemed surprised I was so quick. But it only set him back for a heartbeat, and then he slashed forward again, bringing his knife from his waist up toward the center of my ribs.

I brought the garbage can lid around and managed to shield myself.

His blow was so hard that the knife tore through the metal, missing my hand by inches and stopping just short of my stomach.

He yelped.

It was too late for him. I brought my other hand around, and it caught him on the side of his jaw.

He dropped. I stood above him, heaving for breath, glad to be alive. The man had just tried to put a knife through the center of my body. I steadied myself, ready to go after him again.

Nadia ran forward. "No!" she cried. "Don't!"

Her voice was like a pail of cold water thrown into my face.

I stopped.

He groaned and tried to roll over.

"Please," Nadia said. "Go now."

"And leave you here with him?"

"You have caused enough trouble. Please go." She knelt beside him and cradled his head in her hands.

I stood, unable to understand.

She looked up at me. There was a sad smile on her face. She spoke as if she were many years older than I was.

"Goreela, you are a sweet, sweet boy. I thank you for caring for me. But if you truly care, you will go now. It is the only chance I have."

I turned and stumbled out of the alley.

How could any person make sense out of this, let alone a big, battered hockey player like me whose job never depended on thinking?

chapter thirteen

I couldn't play the next night either—at game time my face still looked like uncooked hamburger. I couldn't see how it mattered. I wanted to be on the ice. Instead I had to watch game four from a seat in the stands, again just up from our players' box.

The night before, I had returned from the knife fight with Mr. Eyepatch to find we were leading 6-3. The game had finished 8-3, putting us up two games to one in the series.

From the start of this game, however, we were doomed. Chandler missed an easy open net two minutes into the game. Then the Russians stormed down the ice to score on a tic-tac-toe pass play that made us look like blundering robots. I could hear my dad watching this in September and yelling his anger at our stupidity for allowing the Commies to score so easily.

The Russians scored four more goals in the next ten minutes. All I could think about was getting back on the ice and throwing my body around. Instead I was forced to sit up here and watch the slaughter.

To add to my lousy mood, I couldn't get comfortable. In this ice arena, the seats consisted of wide planks, barely more than glorified steps. Because the planks weren't divided into one seat per person, Russian spectators pushed and jostled for better positions all through the game. When I stood to cheer our first goal of the night—scored on a deflected slap shot—someone slid over to take my spot, and I had to fight to get my seat back as I sat down.

We scored again a few minutes later. I made the mistake of standing again. This time, when I tried to sit, some woman in a gray shawl had wedged herself almost beneath me.

I decided to pretend I was Russian. I squeezed down beside her and took the space I needed, squishing her into a fat man on the other side of her.

She elbowed me in the right side of my ribs.

I knew I couldn't elbow her back—this wasn't hockey—so I pretended it hadn't happened.

She elbowed me again, and I brought my right arm down to protect my ribs. Then she grabbed my arm.

I turned my head to ask her to let go. She wouldn't understand English, but maybe the sight of my stitched and bruised face would scare her away.

I discovered her shawl pushed back. Nadia!

"Goreela," she said, "watch the game. People must not know we are talking."

I drew a breath to finally correct her about my name. Except I realized Hog wasn't much of an improvement. And so few people called me Timothy that it would sound just as strange to me as Gorilla.

"People?" I asked. "You mean the guy with the knife?"

"Yes. Boris. He cannot know I am speaking privately to you."

I took a quick look at her face again. There was no trace of where he had slapped her.

"Are you all right?"

"Watch the game," she said. "I remind you again. If he knows I am speaking with you, I am in serious danger."

I wondered what spectators around us might think about our conversation, until I remembered they were Russian. The safest thing Nadia and I could do was speak English.

"What is going on?" I asked from the side of my mouth, my face turned back toward the ice. Hadn't she just the night before called me a simple boy and told me to leave her alone?

"He and I had a disagreement that is none of your concern." She paused. "Tell me, what do you expect to gain by betraying Boris?"

I nearly turned my head to stare at her in disbelief. "You think I betrayed the eyepatch guy?"

"You assisted him in Moscow. Then, strangely, you fought him here in St. Petersburg. I cannot really believe you did this because he struck me."

The Russians swarmed our net. Three shots later, they scored to make it 6–2. But I cared less about the game than I had earlier.

"Where I come from, it isn't right to hit a woman."

"I wish I could believe that," she said.

"Believe it," I assured her. Then I asked, "What do you mean, assisted Boris in Moscow? And betrayed him here? Are you sure we're talking about the same guy? The one with the eyepatch?"

"Yes. Boris."

"I did not assist him. I don't even know him."

Sigmund Brouwer

"You and Chandler," she said, "you are together, are you not?"

"Yes," I said. "But it's not what you think."

"You are his bodyguard. Is that the way it is said in English?"

It was very difficult to look at the ice as if I were watching the game. "What!? Bodyguard?"

"The black market in Moscow. It is a place where you can hire murderers. Robbery is as common as shaking hands. With someone as big as you nearby, Chandler has few fears."

"No," I said, "I only did it because..."

Because he had offered me a large sum of money. To walk with him. I guess it did make me a bodyguard, even if I didn't know it at the time.

"Yes?" she asked.

"Nothing. But hanging around with Chandler doesn't make me friends with Boris."

All the time we talked, she leaned into me. I wondered what it might be like to sit this close to her at a movie. I reminded myself that girls like her would not date guys like me.

"I wish I could believe that too," she said, so quietly I almost missed it.

"Please, tell me what is going on." I wasn't good at riddles, and this one was driving me nuts.

"If you already know, I shall be wasting my breath. If you don't know, it is best for you it remains that way."

Another riddle answer. "Nadia, I—"

She squeezed my arm. "I must go before Boris wonders about my absence."

"But—"

"Did I thank you last night for facing Boris? If truly you did it for my sake, I owe you a debt."

With that, she disappeared back into the pushing crowd. Instead of answering questions, she had raised too many more. So why did I have this insane urge to want to trust her?

chapter fourteen

I was allowed to dress for game five. We needed the win badly. By beating us the night before, the Russians had tied the series. Whoever won this game would go up three to two in the best-of-seven series, and with the two remaining games back in Moscow would only need one more win to take the $100,000 prize.

Klomysyk was not dressed to play for the Russian all-stars. It shouldn't have surprised us, though. Since he had ripped my face open and hidden beneath the net, the Russian fans had booed him with their weird whistling every time he'd stepped on the ice.

Maybe losing one of their biggest guys demoralized the Russian all-stars. They skated poorly and made it easy for us to get the go-ahead game with a 7–3 victory.

We were on the return train to Moscow by ten the next morning. This time, however, it wasn't the Avrora high-speed train. Today was an off day. Because there was no hurry to get to Moscow for an evening game, Henley had decided to save some money and put us on the slow train.

This one seemed straight out of a Second World War movie. It clacked and swayed. We traveled second-class, called hardseat because we sat on wooden benches with only thin cushions for comfort.

I had the aisle seat. It was stuffy in the train, so Nathan, in the window seat beside me, had no trouble sleeping. But despite the heat, I couldn't sleep. I was thinking too hard about the events of the previous few days. What was Chandler's game? How was he linked to Boris, the eyepatch man? What was Nadia's involvement? How could I get out of all this?

We passed colorful wooden houses, and I had plenty of time to watch people as they worked in their gardens and fields. Even with the distractions of scenery, I kept returning to my questions until the conductor interrupted my thoughts.

He set a small tray in my lap. The tray held a cup of oily tea, some cream and sugar. We had learned conductors often added to their income by running a small concession business on the train. This tea, however, was a surprise to me.

"I didn't order this," I said.

He said something in Russian. I didn't know if he was disagreeing with me, talking about the weather or insulting me.

"Not mine," I said, slowly and loudly. I gave my head a shake. As if talking slower and louder made it easier for him to understand English.

The conductor wore a black jacket, almost as ragged and dark as his bushy eyebrows. He lifted those eyebrows as he shrugged at me. Then he turned and left me with the tea.

Oh well, I thought, whoever actually ordered this will eventually chase down the conductor. In the meantime, what am I going to do with black Russian tea?

I looked over at Nathan to see if he could be suckered into trying it. He was still asleep.

I decided to dump the tea. When I lifted the cup, I saw a folded piece of paper on the tray beneath it. In neatly printed letters there was a single word: help.

I set the cup back on the tray and opened the note. More neat printing: *Goreela, we must talk. Go ahead to the first-class section. Walk through slowly. Nadia.*

I thought about it. I decided nothing could go wrong here on a train. For lack of anywhere else to put the cup of tea, I carried it with me.

To reach first class, I had to leave this train car and cross through a rattling, bouncing walkway into the next car. I discovered first class was not rows of seats like our car. Instead of the aisle running down the center, it hugged the left side of the car. Door after door ran down the right side of the aisle. All of them closed. Private sleeping compartments?

As Nadia had instructed, I walked through slowly.

Coming my way was a middle-aged man in a brown suit. It would be a tight squeeze getting past him. He waited as I walked forward. When I reached him, he turned sideways and pressed against the windows of the train to let me past. Except as I brushed by he slammed me hard, pushing me against the door to my right. It popped open and I almost fell, catching my balance a couple of steps into the sleeping compartment. Half of the hot tea sloshed over my hand.

The brown-suited man quickly moved into the compartment toward me. Without thinking, I flung the remaining tea into his face and drew my hand back to punch him.

Someone grabbed my arm from behind me.

"Settle down, boy," a voice said with a Texas twang. "You're with friends."

The guy in the brown suit sputtered and cursed as he looked down in disbelief at the dark tea stains on his chest. At least, I guessed it was cursing. He spoke Russian.

The guy behind me didn't let go of my arm.

"You're a big one, son," his drawl continued. "The only way I could stop you is by shooting you, and I'd hate to have to do that."

I relaxed. The unseen man behind me let go of my arm.

Mr. Brown Suit dropped his fast-paced Russian to mere mumbles and vainly brushed at the tea stains.

"Go on, son," the drawl said, "take a load off your feet. Sit down."

I remained standing. The man with the drawl moved around me and locked the sleeping compartment door. Finally he turned to face me.

"Boy, we can be friendly here. Trust me."

He spoke to Mr. Brown Suit. "And Ivan, rest your mouth. All the talk in the world won't get rid of the mess on your suit. Serves you right for being careless, anyway."

I snuck a quick glance around the sleeping compartment. On one side, a low couch. On the other, two bunk beds. In between, hardly enough room for the three of us to stand without bumping into each other. One thing was missing, though.

"Where's Nadia?" I asked.

"She agreed with me that it wouldn't do her any good to be seen with us," the man with the drawl said. He stuck out his hand. "By the way, my name is Clint Bowes."

Slowly, suspiciously, I stuck out my hand and shook his.

Clint Bowes was tall and snake skinny. His hair was greased back, dark brown with strands of gray. His nose was like a popsicle stick turned sideways and stuck into his face. He wore a dark-gray suit, but instead of dress shoes he had on shiny, buffed cowboy boots.

"I'm from the U.S. Customs office," Clint said, a lazy smile across his face as he spoke. "Ivan, my partner here, is from the equivalent government bureau in Russia. He speaks English but prefers not to."

For a greeting, Ivan frowned at me.

Tall as Clint was, he had to reach above his shoulders to place a hand on my shoulders. He tried to press me downward onto the couch behind us. When he failed to get me moving, he shrugged.

"Suit yourself. Ivan and I want to be comfortable."

They sat side by side on the lower bunk bed. Feeling stupid, I finally lowered myself onto the couch opposite them.

"Let's cut right to the chase," Clint said. "You're mixed up in something you shouldn't be. Fact is, until Nadia told us about the fight with Boris, we figured you to be part of their team."

"Do you have ID?" I asked.

"Huh?" Clint's eyebrows dipped as he

squinted at me. "Oh. Identification. You still back on that? Try to keep up with me, boy."

He dug into his suit pocket and pulled out a badge. "Look at it good, boy. See on the front it says U.S. Customs? On the back you'll see my photo. If that isn't good enough for you, I'll leave you a number you can call. Folks at the Moscow bureau will confirm it for you."

"How do I know you're with Nadia?"

"You are as slow as you are big. Think back to the note, son. Did she address it to Timothy? Or Hog, as I understand most folks address you? No, boy, she wrote it to Goreela. I had a devil of a time with that, until she told me it was your name. I didn't have the heart to correct her," he said with a laugh.

I thought everything through. Only Nadia would call me Gorilla.

"Fine," I said. "I'll listen to what you've got to say."

Now his eyebrows danced upward as he gave me a look of mock surprise. "Well, you are considerate, aren't you, boy? Especially facing five years in a penitentiary for what you've already done since you've arrived in Russia. And if you're lucky, you can do those five years back home, instead of in some concentration camp in Siberia."

He grinned at me. "Yup. Siberia. That got your attention, didn't it, boy?"

"I already said I'd listen." I wasn't going to let him push me around.

The train bounced us from side to side as we rounded a bend. I placed a hand on each side of me, gripping the edge of the couch to keep my balance. I waited for him to continue.

"In a nutshell," Clint Bowes said, "you're smack in the middle of a pipeline that has been moving millions of dollars worth of irreplaceable art out of Russia."

chapter fifteen

I hadn't kept up on international art news.

Clint Bowes made up for it, though. Over the next ten minutes he explained— with occasional surly interruptions and corrections from Ivan—that two major events had happened, both in Russia.

In St. Petersburg, the Hermitage Museum had unveiled a treasure trove of Impressionist paintings—a style popular in the 1880s. The paintings had been hidden since being stolen during the Second World War by Nazi war criminals.

And Moscow's greatest museum, the Tretyakov Gallery, had just opened after ten years of renovation. Back in public view were 100,000 pieces of art that covered nine centuries of Russian history.

During the entire time he spoke, Clint Bowes kept his eyes glued to mine. I wondered if he was admiring the stitch pattern made by the Russian doctor across my cheekbone, or if he was searching for any sign that I knew any of this or understood where his conversation would lead.

"What it means, boy," he told me, "is there have been plenty of chances for the occasional piece of art to disappear. Take St. Petersburg. Sure, they've unveiled all this long-lost art. But was there a list of it in the first place? No sirree. Pretty easy to help yourself without a checklist to keep you honest."

He shook his head at how easy it would be to steal the art. "And look at the Tretyakov Gallery. Workmen in and out for ten years. Shoot, for two of those years, what with the money shortages and political mess here in Russia, nobody did anything on it. It just sat there, empty of people. Plenty of opportunities to juggle lists and sneak out canvas paintings, wouldn't you say? Who's going to notice a few missing out of a hundred thousand?"

"I don't understand what this has to do with me," I said. And I didn't. All I'd seen around Chandler was the packet he slipped into the white Mercedes at the black market in Moscow. He hadn't taken anything in return.

"I'll give you the ABCs, boy, and I hope it sinks in. See, this art is worthless until you get a buyer outside of Russia. The States. Europe. Japan. And boy, no one pays for art they don't get placed into their grubby hands."

He watched my face some more. "Don't you get it? Someone has to smuggle money into Russia to pay for the art. And it can't be money in checks. It's got to be cold, untraceable cash. American dollars. Not worthless rubles. And in case you didn't know it, boy, it's a federal offense to carry more than ten thousand dollars in U.S. currency."

He took a breath. "Not only that. Someone has to smuggle the art out to the buyers once it's paid for. That's where your friends come in."

"Can't be," I said. "This is a legitimate hockey tour. It will be a television special and—"

"Boy, you got potatoes growing between your ears. We know you went for a little midnight walk with your friend Chandler Harris. We saw Harris give a small package to a known Moscow art dealer. We're figuring the package held thousand-dollar bills, boy. Hundreds of them."

"Hundreds of thousands?" Chandler Harris had been carrying hundreds of thousands of dollars? No wonder he'd been able to spare me the meager thousand. "But how could you know?"

"Nadia. She's our inside spy."

This was all too much for me. I wanted to be somewhere simple and safe. Like on the ice with guys trying to give me enough stitches to make my face look like it had been run over by a sewing machine.

"I'm trying to lay it out plain for you, boy. Nadia's been the interpreter for this all-star team each year since it started coming over. It wasn't until recently that we realized she's been part of this pipeline of smuggled art. We began to have her followed. Which led us to you and your friend in Moscow's black-market area. It don't take a rocket scientist to figure some of the art is leaving the country with your hockey team. Our question is how. Which is why Nadia is helping us nab the head honcho. We made her the same offer we're going to make you, and I'll get to that shortly. She's working for them—but as what you might call a double agent. She's really reporting back to us."

That explained her strange actions toward me.

"As I've said, Ivan here is my Russian counterpart," Bowes said. "You'd be surprised how closely we work together on these things. We told Nadia to go ahead as if everything was normal and to keep us informed. We want to catch them in the act. It gives us the best chance of recovering the art."

The train's clacking began to slow. We were approaching one of the small towns between Moscow and St. Petersburg.

Clint Bowes looked at his watch. "This is our stop. We don't have much time, boy. I'll tell the rest as quick as I can. Pay attention and try to keep up."

Bowes took another deep breath. He lost some of his drawl as he quickened the pace of his words. "In Moscow, Chandler Harris delivered half the money. A down payment. While your team has been in St. Petersburg, the dealer has been putting together the art shipment. Tonight or tomorrow night, Harris is making the final payment, and at the same time he'll take delivery of the art. You with me, boy?"

I hated being called boy. I hated it when people thought I was stupid just because I was big. I nodded anyway.

"Your job, boy, is to find out two things: how the artwork is going to be smuggled back, and where Harris got the money. It won't do us much good to nail Harris without getting the one who sent him."

"My job?" I hadn't spoken for so long, my words came out as a croak.

"Yes, your job," he said, "unless you want to be sending your folks postcards from Siberia. That's the offer I told you I'd explain. Help us and you buy your freedom. Nadia thought it was a plenty good deal. Course, she's heard plenty on how bad Siberia can be."

"I don't know about this."

"We've got people watching you guys all the time. If something happens, you should be safe."

Should be safe?

He read my mind. "Boy, this is a game involving millions, when people in this country will kill for hundreds. This is not like playing a game of hide-and-seek."

Clint Bowes reached into his suit pocket and pulled out a business card. "In the meantime, as soon as you find out what they've done with the art, call me here.

Don't say anything about it over the phone. We'll arrange a place to meet."

"If I do this," I said, "how do I—"

"Not if. When."

"How do I know what I'm looking for?"

"As near as we can tell, they've got some miniature canvases. Think of a painting no larger than a sheet of typing paper." He paused. "Boy, don't be looking for the frames. Frames are useless. It's the canvas that's worth millions. You can expect a painting will roll up hardly thicker than the inside of a roll of toilet paper."

He forced his business card into my hand. This was all happening so fast I didn't know what to say. Nor did I have the chance.

Smoothly and quickly, they stood together, unlocked the compartment door and stepped outside. From the aisle, Clint Bowes stuck his head back into the compartment.

"Boy, you do understand you need to stick close to Harris now? If you lose him, you might just lose your freedom."

They disappeared.

Great choices. I could try to help the government people and risk my life. Or I could stay out of this and risk my freedom. And if I lost my freedom, I'd lose my hockey career.

All of a sudden I saw too clearly how high the price was on the thousand dollars I'd accepted from Chandler Harris.

chapter sixteen

In Moscow we checked in at the same hotel where we'd stayed earlier. When I got to my room, I found Nathan Elrod unpacking his suitcase on the narrow bed beside mine.

He looked at me and shrugged. "Harris is back to rooming with Hutton."

"Hutton?" Paul Hutton was nearly the biggest forward in the league. I was one of the few guys bigger.

"Yeah. Chandler was probably tired of looking at those ugly stitches across your mug.

And if you haven't noticed, what Chandler wants, Chandler gets."

"What you're telling me is if we learn to score goals by the buckets, we'll get the same kind of treatment?" I was doing my best not to show any concern. How did I have a hope of watching Harris from this hotel room? And was this switch an accident, or had Harris changed his mind about taking me along on his next night excursion?

Before I could say anything further, there was a knock on the door. Because my mind was on Chandler Harris, I fully expected it to be him.

Nathan opened the door to see Nadia standing in the hallway.

"May I speak with Goreela?" she said quietly.

"Wrong room," Nathan told her.

I was already moving past him. "It's for me."

"Goreela?" Nathan asked.

"Long story, Nate," I explained. "Tell you later."

"We can go for a walk?" Nadia asked.

"Sure," I told her.

She looked at Nathan. "Please. Will you tell no one I was here?"

Nathan probably caught the nervousness in Nadia's voice. He pulled me aside and spoke in a low voice.

"Big guy, I'm worried. You haven't been yourself. It's like..." He struggled for words. "Like you forgot hockey is supposed to be fun. What's going on, anyway?"

"Too much," I said. "It's about some money I need to return."

Nathan looked me directly in the eyes. "Remember those long road-trip talks we had back when we played for the Blazers? Stay true to what you believe, bud. If I can help—"

I shook my head. No sense getting him into my trouble. It was nice, though, knowing the help was there. And nice, too, the reminder I needed to be able to live with my conscience.

"He won't be long," Nadia broke in, her voice urgent. "But I need to speak with him."

Nathan nodded.

Sigmund Brouwer

I followed Nadia down the hallway, feeling like a moose trying to keep pace with a ballerina.

At the end of the hallway, she opened the exit door to the same stairs we had taken on a night that seemed very long ago. Without speaking, she led me up to the roof again.

The evening was just beginning to darken, and the Moscow skyline formed box edges against a cloud-covered sun.

"I will talk quickly," she said. "The less I am seen with you, the safer it is for both of us. Those government men. They spoke with you on the train?"

I nodded.

"They are worse than rats." She spit onto the graveled tar of the hotel roof. "I do not trust them at all."

"I don't understand," I said. "They said you were working for them. They said you gave them my name."

"Yes, I am working for them." She raised her head and looked me directly in the eyes.

124

"Yes, I gave them your name, but only because I have decided I can trust you."

"You always could. I told you that."

"Words mean nothing."

"Then how—"

"Did I decide to trust you? After we spoke in St. Petersburg, Boris met with Chandler Harris. Boris took me along to translate. Boris told Chandler he intended to have you killed."

"What?"

"Boris said you could not be trusted."

"What did Chandler say?" I could hardly believe people had calmly discussed whether I should die.

"Chandler said you knew nothing of this. He said he only took you along because you were the strongest person he had ever met. He said you were the perfect bodyguard. Big and stupid."

I thought of how I had lifted Chandler from the airplane seat, trying to make him understand it was a mistake to mess with me. I remembered how he had suddenly become friendly after that and how I had let him lead me along. Chandler was right about one thing: I was stupid.

Nadia's hand was on my arm. "Goreela, I have seen your eyes and how you watch everything. I know you are not stupid."

I smiled so suddenly it almost cracked open my stitches.

"And I know you are not part of this. So you are my only hope."

"Why not the government people? Didn't they promise to help you if you helped them?"

"I believe Ivan wishes to steal the art for himself."

"But he works for the police. And he's got the U.S. Customs guy with him. Clint Bowes."

Nadia sighed. "Goreela, this is Moscow. Do you know what life is like here?"

"Only what I see," I said. Regardless of the subject, I wanted this and any conversation with her to last forever.

"When Boris spoke about having you killed," she said, "he knew it would cost only two hundred dollars. Such is the corruption here, and such is the value of American money. Before, we had the KGB, our secret police. Yes, the KGB did much evil, but it also prevented lawlessness. Now, even the police cannot be trusted. Ivan and his partner, Clint Bowes, can make millions. Is that not enough reason to steal from thieves like Boris?"

"Can't you report your fears to Ivan's boss?"

"His boss may be equally interested in stealing the art. Or Ivan may have me killed."

What chilled me most was the utter certainty on her face. What kind of situation have I gotten myself into? I wondered. How am I going to get out?

"Just so I can be clear, let's see if I understand all of this." I took a breath. "Boris and Chandler are working together to bring money into Moscow and stolen art out. Boris thinks you're working for him, but you're secretly working for the Russian police. Except you think they're equally interested in keeping the stolen art."

Her faint smile of agreement was like a hint of sunshine through rainy skies.

I took another breath. This one deeper. "What is it you think I can do?"

"While I know you are not working with Chandler and Boris, Ivan believes you are. He saw you the night Chandler delivered half the money. I have also informed Ivan you work with them."

"Why?"

"This is important, Goreela. For us to steal the shipment from both thieves—Boris and Ivan—it should appear we are working for Boris, but secretly working for the Russian police. It is why I gave your name to Ivan and the American. Now they think you are a double agent, just like me."

My head felt like it was bouncing around in hurricane winds. We were going to steal the shipment? We were going to double-cross the double-crossers?

I must have groaned out loud.

She looked concerned. She reached up and lightly touched the bruises on my cheek. "Your face? Does it hurt?"

I wished this was a normal conversation about movies and high school and hockey. Then I could have enjoyed the touch of her fingertips.

But I couldn't. Because other questions were forcing themselves into my mind. Pretty girls never go for guys like me. What if Nadia was using me in the same way Chandler had used me and in the same way Ivan and Clint were using me? What if Nadia intended to double-cross me?

"My face is getting better each day," I said in answer to her question. "I'm just glad I can play hockey again."

She gave me a full smile.

All of this had happened because I had let money tempt me into areas I knew were dangerous.

I watched her smile. I smiled back. I knew what I had to do to make things right again.

"Nadia," I said, "tell me what you need from me and, if it's legal, I will do my best to help."

chapter seventeen

We jumped to an early one-goal lead in game six. It almost didn't matter to me. Pumped and ready to play, I still couldn't shake thoughts of Nadia and millions of dollars of stolen art.

I tried and tried to get my concentration back. The Russian crowd was screaming and hollering. The Russian players were skating hard, checking us hard. Our own guys were yelling, grunting, sweating.

I couldn't feel like I was part of it.

My shifts on the ice were mechanical. My body was working on its own, my legs going through the motions, but I had no zing.

From the players' box, I would scan the crowd for Nadia instead of watching the game and cheering for our guys. On the ice before face-offs, I would scan the crowd. Skating onto and off the ice, I would scan the crowd. I didn't see Nadia anywhere, which made it more difficult for me to concentrate.

Double-crossing the double-crossers. I wasn't sure I had the skills to play that game. In hockey, at least, I could depend on size and anger. And in hockey, if you lost, it didn't cost you your freedom or your life.

We went up 2–0 on a power-play goal. The first period should have ended that way, except with less than a minute to go in the period, Chandler Harris made a poor cross-ice pass, which their center intercepted at full speed. He cut between our surprised defensemen, made a couple of moves on our goalie and flipped the puck into the top corner.

The second period started almost the same way. Chandler was daydreaming instead of guarding his man. A pass out from behind the net, a flick of the Russian's stick, the bulging of the net behind our goalie and just like that it was a tie game.

I wasn't doing much better than Chandler. I missed my hits, bobbled passes and generally performed like the average sick slug.

The highlight of my unimpressive playing came with less than five minutes left in the second period. I was waiting at the top of the face-off circle in the Russians' end. I didn't really expect to get the puck. My talent is not in goal scoring. I wasn't the only person on the team who knew that, so the guys only passed to me if they were desperate to find an open man.

This was one of the few times. Nathan feathered me a soft pass, sliding the puck flat along the ice. I had lots of time but thought I had no time. Instead of stopping the puck, then firing it at the net, I went for a glorious one-time slap shot, hoping to redirect it at the net without stopping it.

Nope.

My balance and aim were so poor that I hit

the ice well behind the puck. Worse, I hit the ice so hard my aluminum shaft snapped. The puck sailed past me, harmlessly reaching the far boards. I was forced to drop both pieces of the stick or face a penalty for playing with a broken stick. I left the two pieces at the top of the face-off circle and charged back to the players' box for my spare aluminum stick.

As I skated to the bench, I opened up the ice on my side of the boards. The Russians moved down the ice, tic-tac-toed another perfect passing combination and scored to make it 3–2 in their favor.

As if that wasn't enough torture for me, during the last shift of the third period, the puck popped loose in front of the Russian net. We were still only down by a score of 3–2. No one was within miles of the puck, and I could score to tie the game. I raced toward the puck, cranking my stick back to take another magnificent boomer of a slap shot, one that would make up for my earlier mistake.

Again, I timed it so badly that I hit the ice instead of the puck. This time my replacement shaft remained intact. But I broke the blade of my stick, which went flying much farther than the puck.

The game ended thirty seconds later. As I skated off the ice—series tied at three games apiece—I shook my head in disgust.

How was my stick breaking going to look on television? I could just hear the commentators chuckling about the big ox strong enough to break an aluminum shaft, but too much of a gronk to manage a shot with all that strength.

In the dressing room I pulled out my blowtorch to heat up the aluminum shaft of my spare stick. I needed to loosen the broken blade. It gave me an excuse to keep my head down and avoid looking into the eyes of my teammates.

Chandler Harris, however, threw me a brand-new aluminum stick with a brand-new blade, worth at least ninety bucks.

I told him no thanks, I could get this old one ready for game seven.

He insisted I take the new stick.

I told him no thanks again and began

to apply the flame of the blowtorch to the aluminum shaft of my hockey stick.

Chandler came over and dropped the new stick in my lap and tried for the third time to get me to take it.

That time I did. Mainly because I had a sudden thought that told me exactly where I might find a few million dollars' worth of stolen art.

chapter eighteen

Nadia knocked on the hotel room door exactly on time: eleven o'clock that night. Four hours after our game had ended. Two and a half hours after our team had finished a quiet supper. Two hours after curfew.

She knocked softly. Nathan was asleep and snoring, and I barely heard her although I'd been listening hard for her arrival. I was fully dressed beneath the covers. I slipped out of my bed and tiptoed to the door.

Nathan's nose-blaring trumpet imitation didn't change as he continued to sleep in peace.

"Thank you," I whispered as I opened the door. "I could not do this without you."

"What is it?" she asked as I stepped into the dim hallway. She was in blue jeans, T-shirt and her leather jacket. She could have been anyone in my high school back home. A raven-haired, beautiful cheerleader. Not someone involved in double-crossing double-crossers out of millions of dollars of stolen art.

"Take us to the basement," I said. I didn't want to tell her anything else. In case I was wrong about the stolen art. Or about her intentions.

"The basement of this hotel?"

I nodded. In my back pocket, the pressure of the rolled-up nylon strap I had taken from my equipment bag reminded me I needed my plan to work.

"Why?"

"Let's go," I told her. "You'll see when we get there."

Normally, as a traveling team, we would leave our equipment at the ice arena, especially with a game scheduled there the next day. In Moscow, however, Coach Jorgensen did not trust the ancient padlocks of the dressingroom doors at the arena. He had also explained to us how valuable our new equipment was in a country where most players were thrilled if they could play in skates younger than themselves. So at the end of every game—despite the inconvenience—we lugged our equipment back to the bus and back into the hotel.

We needed a place to air out the sweaty wet equipment, however. Our hotel rooms were cramped and had little ventilation. Coach Jorgensen had made arrangements to use a large storage room in the rear corner of the hotel basement. Earlier in the evening, when we'd unloaded our equipment and spread it out in the storage room, I'd looked for a way to break in.

I thought I'd found it. Trouble was, I was too big to take advantage of it.

That was why I needed Nadia.

She was standing beside me, squinting at the door to the storage room. "Goreela?"

Her voice, soft as it was, echoed. Here in the basement, the concrete floor did not even have the cheap thin carpet found on the upper levels. Dust-covered lightbulbs merely gleamed, barely bright enough to throw our shadows onto the unpainted walls of the hallway.

I pointed upward. This was an old, old hotel, so old it had ventilation windows above the doors. This window was cracked, gray with filth.

"Stand on my shoulders," I said. "You need to crawl through."

"Goreela?"

I'd studied the door earlier. It locked on the inside.

"I'm going to wrap this around your ankles," I whispered as I pulled the strap from my pocket. "I'll push you up, and on your way down the other side it will save you from falling. Once you're in, open the door for me."

She searched my face, then reluctantly nodded. I helped her stand on my shoulders.

I steadied her legs as she reached for the window and wiggled it open. I grabbed her ankles and pushed upward as she started to pull herself up. I held my breath as she began to disappear. It would be difficult for her, crawling forward and then downward. If the other end of this strap in my hands slipped from her ankles, she would tumble down the other side face-first. And that was just the least of my worries.

I eased the strap upward, slowly letting her down the other side. There was a light thump. The pressure on my strap disappeared. I let go, and she pulled it in. Seconds later the door handle clicked and she invited me inside.

I shut the door behind us and locked it.

Nadia was wrinkling her nose. I smiled and nodded and wrinkled mine in agreement. Months of sweat soaked into hockey equipment is not a pleasant odor, especially with an ancient, wheezy furnace pumping hot air into the stuffy storage room.

"We'll hurry," I whispered. I moved to my equipment bag, dropped the strap inside and pulled out the small blowtorch. I lit it, wincing with fear that the hiss of the small blue flame was still too loud.

"Goreela?"

I smiled at her but gave no answer. With the blowtorch in my right hand, I grabbed my spare hockey stick from a pile of sticks in the corner of the room.

She stood beside me and watched, her eyes squinting in puzzlement.

I opened the dial and increased the flame. Then I ran the tip of the flame over the point where the stick blade was inserted into the hollow aluminum shaft. I warmed it for nearly a minute, and when I felt it was ready, I turned down the flame on the blowtorch and set it beside a support pillar in the center of the room. It hissed softly, unheard above the noise of the furnace fans.

"Hold your breath," I said.

Left hand on the aluminum shaft, right hand on the stick blade, I pulled them apart.

Nadia's face lit with understanding. "It must be warmed for the metal to loosen!"

"Exactly. But that's not why I wanted you to hold your breath. I just hope we find what I think we will."

I needed something to muffle sound. From my equipment bag, I pulled out an old towel. I folded it and placed it on the floor.

I held the aluminum shaft like a ski pole and jabbed it downward against the towel. Instead of a loud ringing of metal against concrete, there was only a slight thud. I jabbed the shaft down again, harder.

"Goreela?"

"Keep holding your breath," I said. I was either a genius or an idiot. We'd soon find out which.

Two more slamming jabs of stick shaft onto towel-covered concrete floor.

I lifted the stick and peered into the hollow shaft. I was rewarded by the sight of thin rolled canvas.

"You can stop holding your breath," I told Nadia. "We've just found some of the art shipment."

I shook the shaft and the roll of canvas slid toward the bottom. Enough stuck out that I could gently pull it loose. I handed her the roll.

With great reverence, Nadia pulled it open, as if she were reading a scroll. It consisted of four small canvases, each one painted with daily scenes of Russian peasants.

"This is it," she said. "But how could you know?"

I shrugged modestly. Why else would Chandler try to keep me from removing the blade from this old stick? It was the perfect place to hide rolled-up canvases. He couldn't have known I'd break my other stick shaft and have to use this one.

I shook the aluminum shaft again and felt movement inside. Altogether, we found a dozen unframed, well-rolled paintings.

Chandler had played me for the idiot I was. The previous night—with me stuck in the other hotel room—he'd delivered the second payment of cash and received the paintings. He'd then planted them in my equipment. I would have carried them through customs. If I'd been caught, I'd have faced time in jail no matter how loudly I said I was innocent.

If I'd made it through customs safely, he would simply have stolen my stick at the other end.

Nadia cradled the canvases—millions of dollars worth of canvas and old paint.

I steeled myself to get ready for my second gamble. The first, of course, had been the location of the canvases. The second? What she actually intended to do with the paintings.

"We'll go upstairs to the camera crew," I said. I had thought this through as carefully as I could. If she refused, it meant she intended to double-cross me along with Boris and the government people. "They can film us as we turn the paintings in at the nearest police station."

"Goreela?"

"The camera crew will love the chance for a great news story. And if it makes the news that these were recovered, nobody in the government will be able to make them disappear again. And nobody will be able to make us disappear."

Was she going to pass the test? Or was

I going to have to take the canvases from her and deliver them to the camera crew myself?

Her face broke into a smile. One to fool me into trusting her? Or one because my plan was good?

I didn't get the chance to find out.

Boris—Mr. Eyepatch—kicked open the door and danced into the room, his knife held waist high. He was followed by our promoter, Matthew Martin Henley. Instead of his usual cigar, he waved an ugly black pistol in the pudgy fingers of his right hand.

chapter nineteen

Without thinking, I stepped in front of Nadia to protect her. At the same time, the thinking part of my mind struggled for something to say. Matthew Henley?

Henley smiled and shut the door behind him. "Out of your room after curfew, Burnell? You know that can get you in trouble."

He waved his ugly black pistol to prove his point.

Boris Eyepatch grunted and moved toward me, swishing his knife from side to side.

"Nadia dear," Henley said, "please instruct Boris to relax. I don't like the sight of blood."

I hadn't noticed that Nadia had stepped out from behind me. She spoke quick and low to Boris. Boris frowned but stopped advancing toward me.

I felt like an idiot. Nadia didn't need protection. Not when she was working for both of them.

"This makes for an interesting problem," Matthew Henley said to me. "Obviously you've found the payload I needed you to smuggle back for me."

I was starting to put it together. "Chandler Harris works for you," I said to Henley. "That's why he was able to switch roommates whenever he wanted."

"You are smarter than you look." He snorted. "Of course, that's not saying much."

I felt my fists curl into giant rocks.

"Tut, tut," Henley said. He brought the pistol up until I was staring directly into the hole of the barrel. "Remember, bullets are faster than punches."

I took a deep breath and forced myself to relax.

"That's better," Henley told me. "You just settle down easy. Because we have a little difficulty to straighten out here, and it might take a couple of minutes."

Nadia remained at my side, silent. Boris stood frozen just ahead of Henley. Boris's good eye was unblinking and staring at me— he seemed like a Doberman, straining at an invisible leash and hoping for the command to attack.

"Yes," Henley said. "Chandler works for me. So does Nadia. And Boris. You'll have that choice too."

Was I hearing right?

"Don't get me wrong," Henley said. His fat face was beginning to drip with sweat in the heat of the basement. "When you hear how long it took for me to set this up, you'll understand why I won't hesitate to solve this problem by letting Boris work you over with the knife."

At the mention of his name, Boris licked his lips. I felt like a big dumb pork chop.

"You see, when I visited Moscow to try to set up the first exhibition tour, someone from the Tretyakov Gallery approached me during an embassy dinner party." Matthew Henley wiped his brow with the back of his left hand. The pistol in his right hand remained steady. "It was Nadia's boss, actually. This gentleman explained his predicament. He told me about a friend of his who had dozens of Russian paintings but no way to reach American buyers or deliver the paintings to them. He suggested perhaps a junior hockey team could help, if only there was someone to assist, someone who would not mind an ample gift of hundreds of thousands of dollars. Being the gentleman I am, I offered my help."

Another wipe of his massive brow. His dark blue suit was almost black in places with growing sweat stains. If the furnace down here didn't stop blasting heat, Henley was going to melt.

"It was simple," Henley said. "He would supply the paintings to sell on this end. I

149

would find the buyers on the other end. So that we weren't involved directly, he arranged for Nadia to become the team's translator, and he arranged for Boris to watch and protect the transactions. I arranged for one of my hockey players to carry the money. We both, then, had our assistants, and we both, then, would not have to dirty our hands."

Henley frowned at me. "Until tonight. Do you realize how close you came to destroying the perfect pipeline? I'm going to run this tour year after year. After all, the networks make money from the tour, and they don't suspect a thing. Chandler is the perfect mule to deliver the cash. He and I both thought you were the perfect bodyguard. Until tonight. I'm not even going to ask how you figured this out, because it doesn't matter. What does matter is your answer to my question."

I swallowed. The heat was getting to me too.

"Yes, a question. You have a choice, Burnell. Join my art pipeline and help, or spend the next ten years of your life in a Russian prison."

"Me?" I finally found my voice. "I didn't do anything!"

Henley shook his head. "Maybe you aren't as smart as you look. Didn't Boris and I just catch you red-handed with these valuable paintings? Hidden in your hockey equipment?"

Henley chuckled, causing his chin to wobble drops of sweat onto the floor. "Or did I forget to tell you that Boris was very senior in the KGB? He still has considerable pull in the police system here. He won't mind looking like a hero as he arrests you. And if you should resist arrest? Who could blame Boris for fighting back with that very sharp knife of his?"

Henley studied my face. "I really would prefer you choose to join my team. I could use someone like you on the all-star tours next summer and the summer after. When Chandler's gone, you can throw the games if we need to keep the series interesting."

"What!"

"Don't be a tedious fool. This tour is entertainment. Blow the Russians out of the water and our ratings drop. Let them win to keep it interesting, we get higher ratings. Higher ratings mean higher advertising revenue. Chandler's been great, giving them goals or missing goals for us to make sure this series goes seven games."

Henley reached into his inside suit pocket with his left hand. I expected him to pull out a handkerchief. Instead he withdrew a thick roll of bills.

"Five thousand dollars," he said. "Consider it a signing bonus. You'll get another twenty once you clear customs back in the States. And that won't be any trouble for you."

"No," I said.

"No?" His voice became earnest. "In the last two years, not a single player has been searched at customs. That's the beauty of this tour. Who would think of it as a smuggling operation?"

"I mean no to your offer," I said. The strength of my reply surprised me. But I'd learned that no matter how much I needed the money, it wasn't always worth the price I paid for it. Chandler's money had left me with nagging shame. How much more would I hate myself if I took this money from Henley? And if I took it, till I was an old man ready to die, I'd always have to think of myself as a thief who would sell his soul for mere money.

So I repeated myself.

"No." I remembered Nathan's reminder the night before, and I felt relief making the right choice between right and wrong.

I looked at Nadia as I continued to speak. "You can't buy me. I may look ugly and stupid, but that's better than pretty on the outside and stinking on the inside."

She bit her lip and looked away.

"Nadia," Henley said, "instruct Boris here to do as he wishes with his knife."

Long moments passed. Long moments that surprised me. Nadia had probably been playing me for a fool from the beginning. It wouldn't have surprised me to find out she had intended to keep the paintings herself.

"Nadia!" Henley raised his voice. "Don't be stupid. You're in this too far to consider sainthood now. Instruct Boris here to cut up this stubborn young hockey player."

I felt my fists become giant rocks again. I felt rage growing inside me. If they wanted a fight, they'd get one. It was going to take more than one or two tiny bullets to stop me.

I tensed and waited for the Russian instructions from Nadia to unleash Boris.

The instructions never left her mouth.

The door suddenly banged open.

"This here party has officially ended, folks." The Texan twang belonged to Clint Bowes. So did the shotgun in his hands. "Drop the pistol, Henley, before I drop you."

chapter twenty

Matthew Henley lowered his bulk by squatting and wisely set the pistol on the floor. With a grunt, he straightened.

Boris dropped his knife.

"Much better," Bowes said. His greasy smile widened. "Sure does smell in here, don't it? Hard to say if it's the hockey equipment or you folks."

He raised his voice. "Ivan, why don't you come in and join this little get-together? These boys are harmless as babies now."

Ivan stepped inside. Same dull brown suit. Same dull face. The only thing not dull and boring was the pistol in his hand.

That made six of us. Nadia and I were a couple of steps from Henley and Boris. Henley and Boris were a couple of steps from Bowes and Ivan. Bowes and Ivan were in the doorway.

"I suppose, as an official U.S. Customs officer, I should do something official about this," Clint Bowes said. His tall lean body seemed relaxed, and he held the shotgun loosely, but I couldn't help thinking of him as a rattlesnake ready to strike. "Course, if I did something official, there'd be a mess of paperwork, and I hate paperwork."

He turned his greasy smile to Nadia. "I think what I'll do is confiscate those paintings you're holding in your lovely hands. It'd be doing you all a favor, actually. See, it saves me paperwork, and it saves you all a spell in prison. Can't beat a deal like that, can you?"

"Let's talk about this," Henley said.

Bowes shifted his attention to the fat man in the dark blue suit.

"Talk?"

"Talk." Sweat was dropping from Henley's eyebrows. He had to raise his voice to be heard above the noise of the hot air coming from the furnace. "You might want to think of us as the goose that lays the golden eggs."

Nadia moved so slowly I wondered if it was my imagination. I didn't dare turn my head to see if she was actually inching her way behind my body. As if I could protect her from a shotgun at close range.

Bowes grinned. "I believe I know that story."

"There are plenty more paintings where these came from," Henley said. "Don't kill the goose now when there are more golden eggs than both of us could spend."

"Interesting prospect," Bowes said. "Except I just don't see a way you can guarantee the golden eggs down the road."

"Mutual blackmail," Henley said. "That's the way I've got it set up with the others. Turning me in means turning themselves in. And nobody is anxious to do that, not when the money flows like water."

I felt Nadia brush against the back of my legs. What was she doing?

"Sounds good in theory, my friend. But no thanks. These paintings are enough for a healthy retirement. I don't need to get greedy." Clint Bowes shrugged. "And I figure the best way to keep you guys quiet is to dump your bodies in the Moskva River. Dead men don't tell tales and all that."

Was I hearing him right?

Nadia dropped the canvases she'd been holding all this time.

"Hey!" Bowes said. "Easy on them paintings!"

I looked back and down. Nadia was already on her knees, scooping the paintings toward herself. Or so I thought.

I'd forgotten about my blowtorch. The noise of the furnace had drowned out the slight hissing of the tiny flame of the torch. On the ground behind my legs, at the side of the support pillar, it had been hidden from everyone else.

Nadia kept her back to Henley and Bowes. She used my body as an added screen, and with a quick twist of her wrist she turned the blowtorch flame on full.

None of us understood what was happening until it was too late. She grabbed the blowtorch and tipped it, directing the flare of white-hot flame at the canvas scrolls.

Dry canvas and oil-based paint. Gasoline would not have swooshed quicker. In a racing burst of flames, the canvas scorched to blackness, then fell apart.

Nadia stood. She handed me the blowtorch.

I turned the flame down, then off. Both Henley and Bowes were too stunned to say anything.

Nadia faced Clint Bowes and spoke with a small smile. "Now there is no reason to kill anyone."

Bowes stared at her open-mouthed. Then he spit. "Not yet," he said, glaring. "With these gone, all we can do is call each other names."

He spit again. "But you will be watched. Trust me. You will be watched. We get our share or the pipeline shuts down."

Bowes turned to his partner. "Come on. There's nothing left here worth killing over."

I followed them out.

chapter twenty-one

I held the surprise for my folks until the September night our *East Versus West Shootout* appeared on television. It was slotted to air at 6:00 PM. I had the delivery people arrive with the surprise a few hours earlier.

The truck rumbled up our gravel driveway late in the afternoon. White, undented and clean except for dust from the country roads, it did not appear to be a vehicle that would ever have business at our farmhouse.

Dad looked up from his coffee at the kitchen table. It was his favorite place in the house because he could see wheat fields and the faraway rolling hills through the window. He'd never said so, but I thought it gave him a feeling of freedom, because there were times his face would soften as he stared into the distance. I guessed he dreamed of when he was working the land himself instead of having to hire others and lose most of the profit to paying their wages and the mortgage on the land. It was during those times he seemed more like the man I remembered before the tractor rolled off the side of a muddy hill and broke his back. He had been fun, warm and affectionate. I still loved him, but I loved those memories of him as he was even more.

"Stupid city fools," Dad said. He raised his voice. "Son, you run out there and give them directions."

Dad hated having anyone see him in the wheelchair, even friends. That's why he never left the house. It was unthinkable he would wheel himself to the back porch and actually talk to strangers.

"I'm pretty sure they made it to the right place," I told him.

"Sure," he snorted. "Next we'll need umbrellas on sunny days because cows have learned to fly."

I smiled. This surprise was going to be worth every penny I'd paid.

As the credits rolled at the end of the *East Versus West Shootout*, Dad shook his head.

"Son," he said, "I still can't believe this."

"Which part?" I asked. "That I was able to come home for the weekend to watch this with you? Or that I scored the game-winning goal to take the series?"

He grinned—a rare sight. "No, you turkey. I've always known you're better than you give yourself credit for. I can't believe the television! I thought you were saving all the money you made to start a business some day."

The television. The new, big-screen television with a new DVD player sitting pretty on top. It was so big it seemed to fill half of the tiny living room.

"Oh, the television," I said. I shrugged like it was no big deal. But it was. Dad loved to watch hockey. It was about the only thing that made him happy, sitting in his wheelchair and yelling at players who couldn't hear him. Now, at least, he wouldn't have to roll up close and squint at a small black-and-white screen.

"Not only the television, but the dishwasher and microwave too," Mom said.

She sat beside me on the couch. I could see the gray in her hair and the roughness of her hands from doing too much work.

I shrugged again. "Mom, you deserve a break."

What I didn't tell her was that my next goal was to get them out of this tiny old house. If I played hard this season, maybe I'd get drafted high enough into the NHL to sign a good contract. Then I'd have enough money to bulldoze this house and build them a new one. If I'd learned anything in Russia, it was that a lot of things mattered more than money.

My brother wandered into the living room, a glass of milk in one hand, cookies in the other. He was almost as big as I was but without a squashed nose, a crew cut and the red line of a thirty-stitch scar across his right cheekbone.

"Want to know my favorite part of the show?" he asked.

"Not the part where I threw up in the guy's glove," I said.

"Nope. Where the camera crew filmed that dude at customs."

"Chandler Harris?" I asked. "You liked that part?"

My brother chomped on two cookies. "Won't everyone? I was reading in today's paper this was expected to get higher ratings than Olympic hockey."

I grinned, although Chandler Harris and Matthew Martin Henley probably wouldn't find it amusing. They'd worked hard to make this more entertainment than hockey, and they'd succeeded. But not the way they'd planned.

With the cameras rolling to get some extra footage for the final segment of the television special, our team had marched through the airport in Russia. Rumors about the artwork must have leaked to the authorities because half a dozen customs agents had swarmed us. When they searched Chandler's equipment, they found three paintings rolled up and hidden in the aluminum shaft of his stick. Apparently the art hadn't all fit in my stick. After Nadia had burned the pieces we'd found, Chandler had decided to keep these last three his little secret.

As Chandler was arrested, he began yelling that it was all Henley's fault and he should be arrested too. Henley forgot all about the cameras and exploded in a nuclear reaction of rage, calling Chandler a double-crosser and about five minutes' worth of other names they had to delete from the television special.

Chandler had yelled back about Henley's payments for dumping games, and that's when the hockey world discovered what I'd known but couldn't prove. As a key player, Chandler had missed all those easy goals to make sure the series was close enough to keep the television special interesting.

The result? Major ratings interest in the *East Versus West Shootout*. How often did a person have the chance to watch a scandal as it developed? The commentators had a great time, speculating on-air which goals Chandler had missed on purpose and which ones he'd really tried for.

And I didn't have to worry about what to do with what I'd learned about Henley and Harris. They'd brought themselves to justice.

As for Nadia, she turned out to be okay. She had liked my plan to deliver the artwork to the camera crew after all. And though she never actually told me, I was sure Nadia was the one who leaked the rumors about the art smuggling to the authorities. I'd always have a secret smile whenever I thought of her. She'd risked her life to torch those paintings.

She'd sent me a letter too, one I kept in my wallet and read at least three times a day. Not only did it include an invitation back to Russia, but it had enough sweet stuff in it to let me believe she could fall for a big, battered hockey player.

"Yeah," my brother was saying, "the coolest part was when the big guy in the blue suit spit on the customs guy who was handcuffing him and—"

The phone rang.

"I'll get it," I said, leaving Dad, Mom and my brother to channel-surf the big screen in the living room.

"Burnells'," I said into the telephone.

"I'm looking for Timothy," the voice replied.

"That's me."

"Tim, it's Fred Duluth. I'm an agent in Toronto. I represent about twenty-five NHL players."

I stood up straight.

"I just saw the *East Versus West Shootout*," he said. "You played some great hockey. Better than great. I can see you going a long way in the NHL."

Dad was shouting from the living room. "Who is it, Hog?"

I put my hand over the mouthpiece. "Tell you later," I shouted back. I spoke into the phone again. "That's very nice of you to say, Mr. Duluth."

"Call me Fred." He paused. "Look, I'd like you to sign with me. I think I can get you an impressive contract come the NHL draft."

I was so surprised I couldn't say anything.

He spoke again. His voice sounded worried, like I'd said nothing because I wasn't interested. "Timothy, you haven't signed with anyone yet, have you?"

"Um, no," I answered.

"Excellent. Why don't you promise me you won't until I have a chance to meet with you and your folks?"

"Well, uh—"

"I'm on the first flight out tomorrow morning," he said. "I can meet all of you for lunch. Deal?"

This was happening fast. I thought it through as best I could and decided this was a situation where money had a price I could afford. I figured I could even persuade Dad to leave the house for this.

"Lunch sounds good, Mr. Duluth."

He took directions from me, confirmed the time he would meet us and hung up.

"Dad!" I shouted. "Mom! You won't believe who just called. It was an—"

The ringing telephone interrupted.

"Burnells'."

"I'm looking for Timothy Burnell," the voice said.

"That's me."

"Timothy, my name is John Clarke. I'm an agent in Toronto, and I'm calling because I just saw you on television. You haven't heard from any other agents, have you?"